Her body stiffened in his grasp

"Don't turn away from me," he urged. "Not tonight."

"What are you asking?" she whispered.

"Only that you stay a little longer, just like this. Nothing more, I promise. Just simple human contact on a night when we both need it."

"So you can pretend I'm Annabel?" Frances asked, certain she was right.

Harry shook his head emphatically. "No. I'm fully aware that I have Miss Frances Wilding in my arms, and I'm very conscious of my good fortune."

Frances knew she should resist. It was only the wine, the night, the temporary bond their mutual unhappiness had forged.

But she could not....

CATHERINE GEORGE was born in Wales, and following her marriage to an engineer, lived eight years in Brazil at a gold-mine site, an experience she would later draw upon for her books. It was not until she and her husband returned to England and bought a village post office and general store that she submitted her first book at her husband's encouragement. Now her husband helps manage their household so that Catherine can devote more time to her writing. They have two children, a daughter and a son, who share their mother's love of language and writing.

Books by Catherine George

HARLEQUIN PRESENTS
640—GILDED CAGE
698—IMPERFECT CHAPERONE
722—DEVIL WITHIN
800—PRODIGAL SISTER
858—INNOCENT PAWN
873—SILENT CRESCENDO
992—THE MARRIAGE BED

HARLEQUIN ROMANCE
2535—RELUCTANT PARAGON
2571—DREAM OF MIDSUMMER
2720—DESIRABLE PROPERTY
2822—THE FOLLY OF LOVING

CATHERINE GEORGE

love lies sleeping

Harlequin Books

TORONTO • NEW YORK • LONDON
AMSTERDAM • PARIS • SYDNEY • HAMBURG
STOCKHOLM • ATHENS • TOKYO • MILAN

Harlequin Presents first edition October 1987
ISBN 0-373-11016-2

Original hardcover edition published in 1987
by Mills & Boon Limited

CHAPTER ONE

THE small car nosed cautiously along the narrow, hedge-lined road and the girl at the wheel frowned as she peered through the rain sluicing down the windscreen, half convinced she must have taken the wrong turning at the last crossroads. For more than a mile there had been no sign of any habitation, only high hedgerows and leafless trees.

Admittedly it had been over five years since her previous visit, and then she had travelled by coach and it had been spring, and warm with sunshine. Which was no doubt why everything looked so different now, she told herself firmly, as she concentrated on steering the borrowed Mini Metro clear of the worst of the craterlike puddles.

Her spirits rose considerably a mile or so further on as the hedges gave way at last to walls of honey-coloured stone and the road, such as it was, straightened out somewhat. She gave a sigh of relief as, in confirmation that she was on the right track, a final bend brought her to tall stone pillars flanking wrought-iron gates embellished with linked capital Cs, the cypher of Curthoys Court. One of the gates stood hospitably open and Frances drove through it with care, relaxing once she gained the tree-lined carriageway beyond, which she remembered as winding for more than a mile through wooded parkland before it reached the house.

In her effort to be punctual Frances found she was ahead of herself. With half an hour to kill she looked about for a place to stop, eventually parking under the complex branch system of a giant beech tree, which offered some protection from the downpour. She switched off the ignition and unpacked the picnic lunch provided by her employer, Caroline Napier, grateful for the salad-filled granary roll and plentiful steaming coffee. The food not only helped pass the time, but quelled the butterflies inhabiting her middle region at the prospect of the coming interview. However trenchantly she lectured herself on the subject of keeping calm it was difficult not to feel tense when she wanted the job so badly.

Her eyes grew sombre as she thought of her lack of success so far. Since she had graduated from university in the summer, today's interview was the first in answer to her countless applications for work in her chosen field. If it hadn't been for her stop-gap job at Glebe House looking after the Napiers' four-year-old son, Frances was quite sure she would have gone spare at times during the past few months. Fortunately the Napiers were kind, and by a strange coincidence it was through working for them that she was actually here at this minute, on her way to what hopefully might be her first job as a bona fide archivist.

She poured the last of the coffee and smiled wryly at the thought of the improbable fairy godmother instrumental in getting her the interview. Edward, or Eddy, Napier was an artist of some repute and an altogether noisier, more colourful personality than his solicitor brother, with a habit of descending unheralded on the Napier household for a few days whenever the urge took him—complete with Flynn, his Irish wolfhound, and whatever female he happened to have in tow at the time. The most recent stay had been utter chaos from start to finish.

Even so, life would still have been moderately bearable but for the sudden, unwelcome fancy the artist had taken to Frances. One way and another she had been heartily thankful when red-bearded Eddy had abruptly taken off with his sulky *inamorata* to the South of France 'to paint olive groves and drink wine in the sun'.

Frances was only slightly regretful that she couldn't manage to feel more grateful to Eddy, since he was the one who had coaxed the owner of Curthoys Court to give her the interview. He was an old friend of Harry Curthoys, and when he learned the latter was in need of an archivist prepared to take up residence at the Court for a while, he promptly asked Harry to give Frances first chance at the job before even advertising it. Caroline Napier, frankly amazed by her trying brother-in-law's thoughtfulness, had been very excited when she passed on the news, since she knew only too well how much Frances wanted such a job. Added to which Caroline was also very much aware of how bereft and lonely the girl was feeling these days since Chris Bradley, Frances's boyfriend, was miles away in Edinburgh.

As Frances thought of Chris, which was something she did most of the time, her eyes softened and she took out his most recent letter to read again. It was his usual brief, cheery little note about his work and his hectic social life, telling her to keep her chin up, something was bound to turn up soon and he would see her at Christmas. Nothing very sentimental about Chris, she thought philosophically, nor was he the world's most prolific correspondent, which was understandable of course since he was so busy. Nevertheless, the spate of letters from him had quite definitely slowed down to a mere trickle compared with the first weeks of their separation. She brightened a little as she thought of writing to Chris about her visit to Curthoys Court and telling him all about the interview, whether she was successful or not—but she *would* be successful, she assured herself fiercely. She was willing to work for peanuts, mere pocket money, however little, which might just be in her favour if the owner of Curthoys Court was really as hard up as Caroline Napier seemed to think. And he must be if he needed to open his house to the public to keep it going—even to the point of surrendering his last bastions of privacy in the shape of his famous library and family archives in an attempt to attract more income from parties of students and schoolchildren. Which was where Frances came in, since he needed an archivist willing to work for the pittance which was all he could reputedly afford.

Frances looked at her watch impatiently, anxious to get the interview over, but there were still a few minutes to go. The last thing she wanted was to appear over-eager by arriving too early, though she was consumed with curiosity at the thought of meeting Harry Curthoys. At one time he had featured very regularly in the gossip columns of the popular press, and her father had been prone to voicing strong disapproval of rich young idiots with nothing better to do than cause disturbances in restaurants and make nuisances of themselves. But to an admiring twelve-year-old, Harry Curthoys had been the epitome of glamour and excitement, all the more so because he was relatively local—Curthoys Court was only about twenty miles from the Warwickshire village where Frances lived. She took an avid interest in the young heir, secretly cutting out newspaper photographs and pasting them in a scrapbook hidden in a shoebox in her wardrobe, utterly captivated by Harry's wild mop of blond hair and his wide, white smile. She had been racked with adolescent jealousy by every one of the countless pretty girls photographed with him.

It would be interesting to see what he was like now, though Frances had been very surprised to hear that he was still unmarried. According to Caroline, Harry Curthoys was hard up because, although the house and estate had been entailed on him, his father had left all the money in trust until his son and heir married. Under the circumstances Frances would have expected the fascinating Mr Curthoys to be hotly pursued by every marriage-minded female of his acquaintance, unless, of course, as she had suggested to a stunned Caroline, his preference leaned more towards his own sex.

Frances chuckled at the memory of Caroline Napier's shocked face as she packed the remains of her picnic lunch away and tidied herself up, wondering if Harry Curthoys might be interested to hear that she had been to his ancestral home before, and on more than one occasion. The first time had been as a school prefect in charge of a party of little girls, with no time to stand and stare. Even then the sixteen-year-old Frances had been instantly enslaved by the charm of Curthoys Court, which was smaller and more lived-in than most of the other stately homes in the area.

This same charm had been powerful enough to lure her back alone a few days later, to look over it at her leisure. It had been spring then, very different from today's November gloom, and after the bus had dropped her at the gates she had wandered along the daffodil-lined carriageway to the house like Dorothy on the yellow-brick road, in search of the Wizard of Oz.

The high spot of that particular day, however, had been the visit to the small family church, which was hidden from the house by a dense yew copse. Frances had lingered there alone for some time, looking at the effigies on the tombs of Curthoys ancestors in the side chapel, all of them resting in supine stone piety, hands clasped, faces raised to heaven, and dogs at their feet. Most of them were battered, not just by the ravages of time, but by the attentions of Cromwell's Model Army, and some of the inscriptions were almost indecipherable. But Frances had hovered over them lovingly until her attention was suddenly distracted by a shift in the afternoon sunlight.

Her breath had caught as a shaft of light struck down from a narrow arched window to illuminate another tomb. This one was fenced off by wrought-iron railings, separated also from the rest by composition, artistry, and even the gleaming white Carrara marble from which it was fashioned. In awed silence the young Frances had crept forward in fascination until her fingers grasped the railings, her eyes wide with wonder. Unlike the other stiff effigies, this figure had no look of death. It was a man asleep: young and graceful, reclining in an easy, relaxed attitude with his back turned to her he lay on one side, one knee drawn up, the other leg stretched out, his head in the crook of his arm and a book lying open just beyond his hand, as if he had dropped off while reading. No armour or robes here, but high cuffed boots, breeches, and a shirt with marvellously executed lace at the wrists and deep collar, where his hair fell in dishevelled lovelocks to hide his face. The effect was so eerily lifelike that Frances had been gripped by the certainty that she had only to reach out a hand to touch him and he would wake.

She had gone back during the summer holidays just to visit the tomb again, and her disappointment had been acute when she found the church permanently closed to the public. Too shy to ask the reason, Frances never went to Curthoys Court again, and in time transferred her affections from marble heroes to the more normal, flesh-and-blood attractions of Chris Bradley, the boy next door.

Her face set in determined lines, Frances started the car and set off along the winding carriageway to the house, windscreen wipers working overtime against the pouring rain. It was a chilly, dreary day, no daffodils now, and she shivered as she parked the car in the courtyard and hurried across the bridge that spanned the moat. When she rang the bell of the gatehouse an elderly man opened the door and looked at her in polite query, quite obviously taken aback at the sight of the small, damp figure in trenchcoat and slouch hat.

'Good afternoon,' she said. 'My name is Wilding. Mr Curthoys is expecting me.'

There was a slight pause, then he smiled politely and led the way across an inner courtyard and though the formal garden to the heavy oak door Frances remembered.

'This way, miss, please,' said the man, and ushered her into the small entrance lobby. But instead of continuing into the great hall, as Frances expected, he tapped on a door to the right marked Private and opened it in answer to a voice from inside.

'Your two-thirty appointment, Mr Harry,' the man announced, and showed Frances into a shabby, functional office dominated by a huge, battered desk piled high with papers and ledgers. A tall, slim man in a formal suit rose from behind it and stood staring at his visitor in unconcealed surprise. Frances was conscious of a similar reaction as she saw Harry Curthoys in the flesh for the first time. The two-headed hell-raiser with the reckless smile had undergone something of a sea-change in the years since she had last pasted his photographs in her scrapbook. The man who waved her to a chair after a courteous word of greeting had fair hair, it was true, but it was shorter and more disciplined now, and the narrow, bright eyes held a questioning, assessing look far removed from the laughing challenge Frances remembered so vividly. He sat down again behind the desk, frowning a little.

'*You* are Frances Wilding?' he asked at last, in a light, drawling voice of considerable charm.

'Yes,' said Frances blankly, wondering who else he imagined she could be.

'I'm Harry Curthoys. How do you do?'

'How do you do?'

He leaned back in his chair, fingering his chin. 'Forgive my surprise, but I'm afraid I was rather expecting a *Mr* Wilding,' he said after a pause.

Frances shot a startled look at him. 'Really? But I signed my first name in full.'

'But your handwriting doesn't indulge in loops, Miss Wilding, so I mistook the "e" of Frances for an "i".'

'I see.'

He smiled a little. 'Somehow I took it for granted you were a man, anyway.'

Frances smarted with disappointment, convinced Harry Curthoys was about to turn her down. 'If your interest lies only in men, Mr Curthoys, I won't waste any more of your time and will leave you to the next applicant.'

She rose to her feet, then stood still, arrested by the sudden rap of his, 'Sit down please, Miss Wilding.'

She sat. Harry Curthoys tilted his head back, looking at her down his aquiline nose.

'My interest, as you put it, is not solely in men at all, either professionally or otherwise. I'd say my tastes are fairly normal, really. The reason for my surprise just now was that although Eddy Napier said he knew this history graduate with a passion for archives, somehow or other he forgot to mention you were a girl.'

Frances looked sceptical. 'My acquaintance with Mr

Napier is slight, but I doubt very much that he forgot. His little joke, I'd say.'

'Very likely.' Harry Curthoys studied her in silence for a while. 'Now that we've established the fact that you *are* feminine would you mind taking off your hat?'

Frances minded quite a lot, but since she badly wanted the job she took off her damp felt hat, as requested, revealing close-cropped curling black hair above a face that grew warm as the man opposite looked her up and down. Like a farmer at a cattle sale, she thought, and tried hard to sit still under the bright scrutiny.

'The problem is, Miss Wilding,' he said eventually, 'that I need an archivist who lives in, with the idea of getting the project off the ground as rapidly as possible. Bates and his wife, who virtually run the place, occupy the gatehouse, but I actually live in the house alone, and I rather think there'd be raised eyebrows if I asked you to sleep at the Court, even in this day and age. You're much too young and pretty.'

Frances looked at him, perplexed. 'But should you consider me suitable for the job, isn't there a village where I could put up—a pub, or something?'

'Not, I'm afraid, on the salary I propose to offer you. Which will probably change your mind about the job anyway.' His voice took on a bitter tone as he named the very modest sum Frances could expect if she worked for him. 'Which will give you some idea of why a history graduate with no previous experience was what I had in mind,' he concluded drily.

'Glad of a job at any price.' Frances smiled at him and his eyebrows rose.

'You should smile more often, Miss Wilding,' he said casually. 'Now, shall we establish a few facts? From your letter you seem ideal for what I have in mind, particularly since your special interest lies with the Stuarts. We have quite detailed records of the Civil War period here— otherwise, I warn you, the rest of the stuff is in something of a shambles and needs a fair bit of time and patience to sort out. The point is, would you be interested in the job at the less than lavish salary I mentioned?'

Frances made no attempt to beat about the bush. 'If I can live in, yes. If not, no.'

'I see.' Harry Curthoys stared down at the pen he was rolling between his fingers, then looked up at her. 'If I *can* arrange something I take it you would like to undertake the work?'

'Yes.'

'Then could I just ask one or two questions, Miss Wilding?'

'Of course.'

'Would you mind telling me why a young girl like you is so keen to get a live-in job? We're a bit off the beaten track here, you know. Not much in the way of entertainment.'

'I prefer to be away from home,' she explained, 'either in a job that pays enough for me to have a place of my own, or something on the lines of what you're offering. To be frank, I've been applying for jobs ever since I graduated and so far I've been unlucky, which is why I've been with the Napiers, looking after their small son. That's how I met your friend, Edward Napier. But young Sam will be starting school after Christmas, and they won't need me any more.'

'Why exactly are you so desperate to get away from home? Are your parents unkind to you—forgive me for being personal.'

Frances shook her head, smiling. 'Not at all. And my parents aren't in the least unkind to me, quite the reverse. My father's been a widower for years, then recently he married again. Jasmine—Jassy to us—is a research chemist, like my father, beautiful as well as clever, and they're both idyllically happy, but——'

'But you feel a trifle extraneous at the moment.'

'Exactly. They need time to get over the honeymoon stage.'

Harry Curthoys smiled. 'Doesn't take long for some people!'

Frances shook her head. 'I'm willing to bet it will for Dad

and Jassy. Not,' she added hastily, 'that they're pushing me out, far from it. In fact Jassy's got quite a thing about the wicked-stepmother syndrome. But personally I think it only fair to give them time alone together, which is the way I shall want it when I marry.'

'Which brings me neatly to the next question.' He hesitated. 'Since you are a girl,' he went on with care, 'surely there must be some male in the offing somewhere who's likely to raise objections if you live here?'

'I do have a boyfriend. Chris graduated in the summer, like me, but he's an accountant and got snapped up by an Edinburgh firm even before he'd qualified.'

'Edinburgh, eh? A fair trip for a date with his lady-love!'

'I don't expect to be seeing very much of him for a while,' said Frances. 'Not before Christmas, anyway. My private life would present no problems, Mr Curthoys.'

'Fair enough. Can you type, by the way?'

'Yes. My father paid for a six-week course for me during the summer.'

Harry Curthoys nodded approvingly, then sat for a while in silence, obviously thinking hard. Eventually he jumped to his feet.

'Look—can you hang on here for a few minutes? I shan't be long.'

'Yes, of course.' Frances waited a little after the door closed on the tall, slim figure, then got up to peep through the small window, just in time to see him disappearing into the gatehouse. She sat down again, conscious of how badly she wanted this job, how much she wanted to work in this beautiful house, occupied with the past she loved so much, and even getting paid—a little—to do so.

Frances clenched her hands in her lap and sent up a silent prayer that Harry Curthoys would find some way round the problem of her sleeping arrangements. It was rather surprising that he considered it any impediment at all in present-day society. But presumably he occupied a fairly feudal position in the local hierarchy, in which case a single girl living under his roof, no matter how innocently employed, would probably be the subject of adverse comment in certain circles even today.

Frances looked up, her tongue anxiously between her teeth, as the outer door banged and Harry Curthoys came back into the room followed by an elderly woman with a kind face and a frankly ample figure swathed in a flowered overall.

'Miss Wilding, this is Mrs Bates, my housekeeper,' he announced and sat down again behind the desk.

Frances smiled diffidently and said, 'How do you do, Mrs Bates?'

The woman regarded her steadily for a moment or two, then nodded and smiled warmly. 'Very well, miss, thank you.' She glanced across at her employer. 'I'll just bring in some tea then, Mr Harry.'

His answering smile was brilliant, reminding Frances vividly of the old newspaper photographs. 'Thanks, Dolly—any scones?'

The woman chuckled as she went out, and Harry Curthoys let out a sigh of relief.

'I think the problem's solved, Miss Wilding, subject to your consent. My housekeeper has just given the gold seal of approval to your tenancy of the guest-room at the gatehouse, which means you can work and eat over here in the Court, then sleep the sleep of the chaste under Dolly's roof at night. Would the arrangement appeal to you?'

'It sounds ideal,' said Frances, rather amused at being vetted by the housekeeper. 'What would have happened if Mrs Bates had given me the thumbs down?'

He gave an apologetic shrug. 'I'd have had to think again. Dolly's been here for ever—she was in charge of the nursery originally, then graduated to head cook and bottle-washer once my father died and the staff had to be drastically reduced. I'm still "Mr Harry", you notice, whereas my father was never anything but "sir" or "the master" to all his staff to the day he died. The staff was a sight more numerous in his day, too.' His face darkened and he changed the subject by asking when Frances could start.

'I'd like to give the Napiers at least a week's notice.'

'Make it two, which will bring us up to the twenty-third. Does that suit you?' He got up and came round the desk, and Frances rose, holding out her hand

'Thank you, Mr Curthoys. I'll be here at nine then, on the twenty-third.'

Harry Curthoys grinned disarmingly. 'No need to shake hands yet—you haven't had Dolly's tea.'

Frances felt an electric tingle of excitement run through her as she finally realised this was actually going to happen. She really *was* going to work here at Curthoys Court. She followed her new employer across the entrance hall and Harry Curthoys threw open the doors of the great hall, whistling softly as he caught sight of the newly lit log fire in the large, carved stone fireplace emblazoned with the coat of arms of the Curthoys family over the mantelpiece.

'I say, you are honoured. Dolly's put tea in here. Not her usual practice, I might tell you.'

'I *am* honoured,' said Frances with sincerity, and gazed about her in delight at the lofty, beautiful chamber, which despite the grandeur of the massive oak chests beneath the windows, and the portraits and priceless Brussels tapestries on the panelled walls, was wonderfully welcoming. Deep, hide-covered chairs were drawn up to the great hearth with its leaping flames and piled log-basket, and the low table nearby was laden with Mrs Bates's version of tea.

The lady herself appeared at that moment and held out her hands for Frances's coat.

'That looks very damp to me, miss. Let me take it to dry off in the kitchen while you have your tea.'

Feeling a little self-conscious in the plain sweater and skirt she had chosen as suitable interview wear, Frances sat down before the tea tray in response to her host's wave of the hand. The tray was enormous, and besides the silver tea service and fragile Coalport china, boasted the promised scones, still warm from the oven, butter, jam, cream, a Dundee cake encrusted with almonds and a plate of toast fingers spread with Gentleman's Relish. Frances regarded the array with anticipation, realising she was hungry, when Harry Curthoys snapped his fingers suddenly.

She looked at him questioningly.

'Your eyes,' he said, and helped himself to a scone, spreading it liberally with jam and cream.

'Yes?' prompted Frances warily, as she began to pour tea with rather more composure than she actually felt.

'Tortoiseshell,' went on her host conversationally, and licked his fingers inelegantly before putting several pieces of toast on his plate. 'When you first opened your eyes fully just now I could see little light streaks in the brown irises— very unusual.'

Frances giggled spontaneously, and relief spread over her companion's face as he heard it.

'That's better,' he said in approval. 'You really should smile more often, you know. You looked positively forbidding when you arrived.'

'I was nervous, and a bit put out because you seemed to want a man,' she said defensively.

'I wish you wouldn't keep on saying that!'

Frances chuckled again, and nibbled some toast. 'Very sorry, Mr Curthoys.'

'That's another thing.' He leaned forward and held out his cup for a refill. 'I answer to Harry much better than Mr Curthoys.'

She eyed him doubtfully. 'Do you think that's suitable, since I'm an employee? Perhaps I could call you Mr Harry like Mrs Bates.'

He took the cup of tea from her and sat back, shaking his head emphatically. 'No way—because I'm certainly not calling you Miss Wilding, Miss Wilding, unless you're hellbent on the idea, of course!'

She laughed, feeling unexpectedly relaxed in the company of this casual, charming man, who was nothing like her preconceived idea of him. 'If you prefer it then, of course, first names it shall be.'

'Good. In any case, this employee business is a bit far from the mark really. If you can sort out all the family records in return for the pathetic salary I'm paying you, I see the arrangement more in the light of a personal favour from a friend.' His eyes lit with a cajoling gleam. 'I don't suppose you'd care to have a shot at cataloguing the library while you're at it, Frances?'

'With pleasure.' The more time she could spend at Curthoys Court the better, as far as Frances was concerned. She cast a hungry eye at the fruitcake. 'Could we start on that, do you think? It looks delicious.'

'That's why it's here. Dolly will be mortally offended if we send anything back untasted.' He frowned at her. 'Did you have any lunch?'

'Not much. I was a bit nervous, as I said.' Frances sampled the cake with appreciation.

'Good grief—of me?'

She gave him a very direct look. 'I've made dozens of applications to anyone remotely likely to need the services of an archivist, Mr Curthoys——'

'Harry.'

'Very well. Harry. They all turned me down. Which is why I was not over-confident when I drove through your gates this afternoon.'

'And you were depressed because your man had gone off and left you, too, I expect?'

'Not left me. Merely gone to work in Edinburgh,' she corrected, and he smiled in apology.

'I'm not renowned for my tact, Frances. You'll need to make allowances for me.'

Frances was fairly sure that most people would forgive this man almost anything, and had done so all his life, except, possibly, the father who had put such stringent conditions on his heritage.

'I'll keep it in mind,' she told him.

'By the way, don't come early on the twenty-third,' he said suddenly. 'It's a Sunday, and the one day of the week at this time of the year I try to have something of a lie-in.'

'Of course. Shall I start the following morning?'

'Is it out of the question to come later on the Sunday? If

you came in the afternoon I could show you the ropes, see if you want anything moved. Bates can tell Mason, the gardener, and one of his lads will supply the muscles. Then we can have dinner together and you can make a start on the Monday morning while I'm away at my office in the town. I'm a working man during the week. I only wear my landowner hat at weekends.' There was a wry quality to his smile that touched a chord somewhere deep inside Frances, and she smiled shyly.

'That sounds fine. Sunday the twenty-third, then.'

'Come about two, while there's still a bit of light, and I'll show you over the house,' he suggested. 'Now I think I'll have another slice of cake.'

Frances cut it and put it on the plate he held out.

'Actually I've been over your house before,' she confessed. 'More than once.'

Harry's thin face lit with interest. 'Really? When was this?'

'I came in charge of a party of little schoolgirls when I was a prefect. I was the one with the printed list of information, reading out the objects of interest with one eye, and watching no one broke anything with the other.'

He chuckled. 'You said visits in the plural, so presumably you came back.'

Frances sat back in her chair, a little drowsy from the heat of the fire. 'I came back twice afterwards on my own. The place had an extraordinary fascination for me, particularly the church. But when I came back the last time the church was out of bounds to the public and I didn't come again. I used to dream about the tomb of the sleeping man. It was so hauntingly beautiful I couldn't get it out of my mind. Why did you close the church?'

Harry's mouth went down at the corners.

'You hit on the right word when you said haunting. An elderly lady got shut in the church by mistake after the house was closed for the day. She almost died of fright before her friends realised she was missing. She swore that the effigy rose and stretched like a man waking up and she passed out from sheer terror.'

'Did he turn round?' asked Frances involuntarily.

Harry stared at her in wonder. 'My dear girl, it's a marble effigy. It neither got up, turned round nor danced a Highland Fling! The whole episode was in the fevered imagination of an elderly, panic-stricken lady, but the incident roused so much public interest I refused to open the church to the public after that. I needed the money— still do—but not so badly I cared to have my home turned into a peep-show for sensation seekers because of Hal Curthoys.'

'Wasn't he the one who fought in the Civil War?'

'The very same. You *have* done your homework!' Harry jumped up to kick a log back into the heart of the fire, and stood staring down as the flames curled round the dry beechwood.

'What happened to him?' asked Frances. 'The book said he died not long afterwards.'

'He just died. No one was able to explain it at the time. An eye-witness account says he ate a large meal and wandered out into the June sun to read in the rose garden at the back of the house. He took off his jerkin and lay down in shirt and breeches to read. Some time later his wife went to look for him and found him asleep. Only he wasn't asleep. He was dead. I suppose it must have been a coronary, a heart attack, but in the opinion of the time it was felt that God—or the devil—had called Hal to him one hot afternoon. His beautiful grieving widow immediately commissioned the tomb and had it put behind bars in the church, where it has stayed for three hundred years. When I opened the church to the public, Hal enjoyed a brief burst of notoriety again. But not any more. The church is no longer used for services, and Bates, who is not given to flights of fancy, cleans the place once a week and that's that.' Harry turned a sober look on Frances. 'And if you don't mind I'd rather you gave the place a wide berth yourself. I don't want any more incidents like the last one on my conscience.'

Frances felt a pang of disappointment, but kept it to herself. 'Were you named for Hal Curthoys?' she asked.

Harry grinned. 'Yes. My father had no truck with superstition. Against my mother's wishes I was christened Henry—the first Curthoys since the unlucky Hal to bear the name, but always known as Harry, at her insistence.' He sighed. 'I miss her a lot.'

'Has she been dead long?' asked Frances gently. To her surprise she received a broad grin in response.

'She's not dead, Frances. After my father died she went on holiday to the States, where she met and eventually married Dexter Bancroft, a retired lawyer, who makes her very happy. My only regret is that I don't see as much of her these days as I'd like.'

Frances smiled and rose to her feet, rather dismayed to find it was later than she thought. 'I must go, Mr—Harry. I promised to get back for Sam's bath-time and the nightly boat-race. I won last night, so he's thirsting for revenge.'

Harry chuckled, and rang for Mrs Bates. 'You like children, Frances?'

'Better than some of the adults I know!'

'Do you want some of your own?'

'Chris and I won't be able to set up home for a fair time yet, but when we do I hope to have two or three.' Frances laughed. 'Boys, preferably, after Sam, because he's so gorgeous. Blond and blue-eyed and so angelic-looking no one believes what an imp of Satan he really is!' She turned as Mrs Bates came hurrying into the room with the now dry trenchcoat. 'Thank you so much, Mrs Bates. I gather you're willing to put me up while I work for Mr Curthoys.'

'It will be a pleasure, miss. Would you like to see the room now?'

'That's very kind of you, but I'm in a rush to get back to the little boy I look after. I promised, so I mustn't be late. And I'm sure the room will be lovely, Mrs Bates, even without seeing it.'

Mrs Bates withdrew as the master of the house saw his new archivist to the door and walked with her through the gathering dusk to the courtyard beyond the gatehouse where Caroline Napier's Mini Metro waited. Harry stood as Frances unlocked the door and got in, then bent as she wound down the car window.

'I hope you'll be happy working at Curthoys Court, Frances Wilding.' He looked down into her upturned face and smiled. 'Do you think you will?'

'I know I will,' she said simply. 'I only hope you'll find my work satisfactory.'

She smiled at him and reversed the car until it was pointing in the right direction, and for the first long straight stretch of driveway each time she glanced in the rearview mirror she could see the slim figure of Harry Curthoys silhouetted against the lights of the gatehouse, as he watched her drive out of sight.

CHAPTER TWO

THE time before Frances's departure from the Napier household went by like lightning. Sam was inconsolable at first and took a lot of coaxing round, but was eventually won over to the opinion that big boys like him didn't need a nursemaid to look after them, though he reminded Frances a dozen times a day of her promise to visit him at Christmas. She wrote at length to Chris, who wrote back congratulating her on her new job, and waxing very enthusiastic on the subject of his own. He was sharing a flat with a fellow accountant from his firm and enjoying his life in the beautiful city of Edinburgh very much. There was so much to do and see, he wrote, and a fair amount of studying to get through somewhere along the way, but he missed her, looked forward to seeing her at Christmas, and in the mean time wished her lots of luck with the new job.

After a painful parting with young Sam, Frances spent a couple of days with her father and Jassy, both of whom did everything they could to include her in the charmed circle they inhabited so blissfully together. Matt Wilding teased his daughter about the suitability of Harry Curthoys as an employer, warning her of the dangers of living in close proximity to a handsome rake of Harry's mettle, even if he had reformed.

Jassy quite openly said that Harry Curthoys sounded rather nice. She gave Frances a new scarlet sweater to wear under the sheepskin jacket bought by Matt for his daughter, so that Frances felt well equipped for her new venture when they drove her to Curthoys Court on the foggy November Sunday afternoon.

Jassy adored the place on sight, her eyes brightening even more when Harry Curthoys emerged from the gatehouse, dressed in an old shooting jacket and moleskin trousers. She and Matt were quite obviously content to hand Frances over to him.

Harry smiled at Frances in friendly fashion as he picked up her suitcases and took them into the gatehouse. 'Feel a bit strange now your people have gone?'

'Not in the least,' she assured him. 'I'm used to goodbyes. I had to board at my school after my mother died, so I learned to be independent quite early.'

He made a face. 'So did I, only I went away to school when I was eight. I don't know who cried more, my mother, my sister Charlotte or me.'

Mrs Bates appeared, scolding as she saw Harry carrying the cases. 'Put them down at once, Mr Harry. Bates will take them up in a minute. I'll just show Miss Wilding her room, then she can come straight back to you before the light fades.'

'Right, Dolly. Take your time, Frances,' he added casually, and strolled back across the inner court, leaving Frances to follow her new landlady up the narrow stairs to the upper floor of the gatehouse.

'Bates and I sleep in the front room overlooking the park,' said Mrs Bates as they reached the landing. 'Here's the bathroom, and this will be your room, overlooking the inner court and house. I hope it will suit.'

As she stepped into the room Frances was able to assure Mrs Bates with complete sincerity that it was everything she could wish for; sprigged curtains and bed cover, Victorian pine furniture, and two latticed windows framing views of the house and inner garden. 'It's charming, Mrs Bates. I shall be very happy here.'

Mrs Bates smiled, gratified. 'Thank you, Miss Wilding——'

'Won't you call me Frances, please?'

'I don't know that I should do that. Mr Harry might not approve. Now you'd best get back to him, because he doesn't have much spare time, poor boy.'

Frances hurried back across the courtyard to the big oak doorway of Curthoys Court. She pushed it open hesitantly, before crossing the entrance hall to peep into the great hall, where Harry was sprawled in a chair near the fire, surrounded by Sunday papers. He sprang to his feet as he caught sight of her.

'Right then, Frances Wilding. Let's get on straight away, shall we, then we can get back to the fire and have tea.'

Hands thrust in the pockets of the long Aran cardigan added to her sweater and skirt, Frances accompanied him with anticipation, rediscovering the house with all the pleasure of renewing acquaintance with an old friend. Harry took her up the stairs at the end of the hall first, through bedrooms which each had a different history—and a red silk rope looped at one side, ready to stretch across when the house was open to the public.

Harry's own private rooms were in a small wing closed to visitors, and he led her past it to a gallery lined with portraits under a barrel-vaulted ceiling. They arrived finally in a solar with a beautiful carved fireplace, and oak panelling lining its stone-faced walls. Beyond lay a spiral staircase leading up to the attics. Harry produced a torch from his pocket when they reached the first of them, and led Frances into a long room very inadequately lit by a single electric light bulb hanging naked from a cord.

Frances stood rooted to the spot in wonder at the sight of deed boxes, tin trunks, cardboard cartons crammed with papers, more tied up in great bundles, old ledgers, everything stacked haphazardly any old way. To the lay eye it was daunting dusty chaos, but Frances gazed with glistening eyes, and gloated.

'Never been touched?' she breathed, not looking at the man beside her.

'Virgin territory. Untouched by human hand, at least for years. I wouldn't answer for the attentions of mice and birds, though. Some of the stuff may be in a pretty grim condition.'

Frances drew in a deep breath of pure bliss. 'I shan't mind.' She glanced about her doubtfully. 'The light's not terribly good up here, though.'

Harry turned off the light, then switched on the torch and put a hand under her elbow to lead her back down the spiral stone staircase. 'I must make one condition, Frances. For the time being I'd prefer you to work in the attics in the mornings only. You get a decent light most days until about one-ish—comes from the window you didn't even notice at the end.'

'No, I didn't. Who would with that treasure trove staring them in the face?'

He laughed. 'Come on. We'll have a quick look round the downstairs rooms, then I'll get busy with the toasting fork.'

The great hall took up a large proportion of the ground floor. Otherwise there were the kitchens, the formal dining-room, a morning-room which Harry kept as a private sitting-room, and after it the coffin room.

'Coffin room?' Frances said, startled.

'They used to keep the dead there until they were buried. Now it's about to undergo a transformation and become the muniment room because it's next door to the library here.' And Harry threw open the door of what, to Frances, was one of the most beautiful rooms in the house. 'This was done by Edward Curthoys, about 1756. It's said to be one of the most perfect examples of early Gothic in these parts.'

The room was lined with oak shelves surmounted with carved finials, and filled with leatherbound volumes side by side with modern novels and books of every description. In the deep, square bay window twin terrestrial globes flanked a tooled leather-topped desk, and in the centre of the room, on the exquisite Savonnerie carpet, stood an oval table and four chairs with *grospoint* seats.

'But this is not open to the public?' asked Frances.

'Not yet. I need a catalogue and inventory done first.' Harry thrust a restless hand through his thick fair hair. 'I need so many things. Sometimes I feel like Canute trying to order back the tide. But don't let me bore you with my problems.'

'Mr Curthoys—Harry—I think I should tell you Mrs Napier gave me some rather personal details about you before I came. About the money being tied up in some way until you marry, I mean.'

'And you can't help wondering, in common with a lot of other people, why I haven't galloped full pelt to the altar with the first obliging female just to release the money.'

'It's absolutely none of my business, but, well, it does rather seem the logical thing to do.'

'Are you offering yourself for the sacrifice?' he asked, eyeing her with interest.

She swallowed hard. 'No, Mr Curthoys, I'm not. My marriage plans are cut and dried already.'

Harry laughed and flipped another muffin on a plate. 'I was only teasing, Frances—I rather enjoy seeing those striped cat's eyes of yours pop open at me. Unfortunately it's a little more complicated than that. I'll tell you all about it some time. Mind you, I once very nearly persuaded a lady to take the plunge, but she changed her mind at the eleventh hour, as it were. Very embarrassing it was, believe me.'

'I feel for you,' said Frances in a heartfelt tone.

He looked across at her musingly. 'You know, I think you really mean that.'

'I do.'

'You're a nice litle thing, Frances Wilding. We'll get on well together, I think.'

When she was unpacking later Frances gave herself a mocking smile in the swivel mirror of the pretty dressing-table. So Harry Curthoys thought she was a 'nice little thing', did he? Rather a put-down, not that it mattered. He was rather nice himself, if it came to that. Not nearly as good-looking as Chris, of course, who was dark-haired and heavily built and would make two of Harry Curthoys. In fact, feature by feature, there was nothing strikingly good-looking about her employer at all, which made it odd that the impact of his charm was so immediate. His light drawling voice and sharply cut features were nothing wonderful, yet when added to his slim, wiry physique and flippant, whimsical manner, it was very easy to see why women found him so irresistible. And yet no one had snapped him up, despite the inheritance that apparently came with him automatically once the knot was tied. Very odd.

Frances curled up on the bed with the pillows stacked behind her and began to write to Chris, giving him her first impressions of the place and scribbling at length about the tangle of records she'd been presented with to unravel. She finished up by telling him she was about to dine with her new employer, who was very charming and friendly, even though she couldn't help wishing Chris were her dinner companion instead.

To her rather guilty surprise Frances found this was not entirely the truth when she was facing Harry Curthoys across a small table near the fire in the morning-room later that evening. She was quite happy to be in his company. Mrs Bates had wheeled in a heated trolley containing the food, served them with soup, then left them to help themselves to the rest.

'I find this the best arrangement, from my point of view and hers,' he explained. 'I'd rather she didn't hang about fussing over me, and I just put everything back in the trolley afterwards and wheel it out to the kitchen for her to deal with the following morning.'

Frances regarded him with some amusement. 'You've just shattered my illusions, you know. I'd never imagined the scion of an ancient family dashing about with a dinner trolley!'

Harry laughed. 'You'd have been much more impressed with my father, he was the ultimate autocrat. Wouldn't have been seen dead doing anything so *infra dig*, I can assure you.'

Frances put their empty plates back in the trolley and took out the joint of beef and dishes of vegetables for the next course.

'You know, it's rather nice to have company at the dinner table,' went on Harry as he began to carve. 'Not that

I'm home every night, of course. I get invited out quite often and a fair amount of my business is done socially over a meal.'

Frances took her plate from him and helped herself to buttered parsnips and roast potatoes, adding Mrs Bates's splendid gravy and a slice of Yorkshire pudding. 'What about my time off, Mr—Harry?'

He shot her a surprised look. 'I hadn't given it a thought. Evenings and weekends at the very least, and if you want more I'm sure we can come to some amicable arrangement.'

'Would you prefer me to be away every weekend, or could I just stay at the gatehouse sometimes?' she asked diffidently.

Harry Curthoys put down his knife and fork and leaned forward to look into her face. 'You can stay here all the time, if you want, Frances. I just assumed a young thing like you would *want* to be away to the bright lights at the first opportunity.'

'Not really. Not much fun without Chris, to be honest. And it's not the back of beyond, I like it here. Besides, it's only a temporary job really, isn't it? When do you reopen the house to the public—Easter?'

He nodded.

'Then I should have something for you to put on display by then, if it's only one particular period, like the seventeenth century,' said Frances with certainty.

Harry looked delighted. 'That would be marvellous. If you could just manage something about the Civil War it would be a help.'

'I'm sure I can safely promise that. I'm an enthusiast on that particular period. I always felt a sort of love-hate reaction to both Charles I and Charles II. They were so different. And one can't help admiring Charles I if only for his dignity at his execution.'

'"He nothing common did or mean upon that memorable scene". I remember doing that poem in school.' Harry grinned at her. 'I particularly liked the bit "when he the axe's edge did try".'

'Ghoul!' she retorted.

She took a hot blackcurrant pie from the trolley and a platter of cheese from a small table nearby and looked at Harry queryingly. 'Which would you like?'

'Both. But you're not here to wait on me, Frances.'

'I don't mind.'

'I shall get spoilt,' Harry remarked. 'I'm not used to all this attention.'

Frances gave him a sceptical look. 'That's stretching things a bit far, Mr Curthoys. Would I be impertinent to mention that I used to read bits in newspapers about you once upon a time? I'd say that whatever else you've lacked in life, attention wasn't on the list!'

His face took on a comic look of dismay. 'Unkind! You shouldn't believe everything you read in the papers, you know. And I've been trying so hard to make a good impression, too. I didn't realise my much-maligned reputation had already upset the applecart for me.'

'It didn't. When I was twelve or so I thought you were too glamorous for words.'

'Glamorous! Ugh!' He looked at her from narrowed eyes. 'And now?'

'You've changed a lot since then.'

'Isn't that the truth! I feel centuries older—though probably not that much wiser.' Harry got up and wheeled the trolley to the door. 'Sit by the fire, Frances. I'll be back in a minute.'

'Oh, but couldn't I——'

'No, you couldn't. Sit.'

He grinned and went rattling of into the distance while Frances stretched out in the deep chair, wondering what his lady-love had been like. His fiancée had been a bit stupid to turn down Harry Curthoys, Frances felt. He wasn't Chris, of course, but she enjoyed his company very much, none the less.

When the door opened it was Mrs Bates, bearing a tray of coffee. 'I thought I'd wait until you'd finished for once tonight, Miss Frances. Mr Harry's on the telephone. He won't be long—says you're to pour out.'

'Thank you.' Frances smiled warmly at her. 'That was a delicious dinner, Mrs Bates.'

The woman smiled, obviously pleased. 'I'm glad you enjoyed it. Now, I'm to give you breakfast at the gatehouse because Mr Harry goes out quite early as a rule. What would you like?'

'That's very kind of you, but I don't eat much breakfast. Toast and tea will do, honestly.'

'No wonder you're so small,' said Mrs Bates in disapproval. 'Never mind, I'll bring you a nice bit of lunch in the library when you've finished in the attics tomorrow. Mr Harry says you're not to stay up there after one.'

'And Mr Harry means it,' said that gentleman as he came in. 'See she keeps to it, Dolly.'

'I will, never you fear. Goodnight, Mr Harry. Goodnight, Miss Frances.'

Harry looked at Frances with mock awe after Mrs Bates had gone. '"Miss Frances", no less. You're honoured. When Annabel—the lady I almost managed to drag to the altar—stayed here she was always "Miss Hayward". Dolly's a stickler for etiquette and all that.' He stretched out his long legs with a sigh, looking rather weary. 'I won't see you until tomorrow evening, so ask Bates for anything you need, and if we don't have it he can ring me and I'll bring it home.'

'I'll need a portable typewriter in time, but not until I have some sort of index to list. I'll need to get things together for a while first.'

They chatted companionably for over an hour. Harry gave her a rundown on the routine of the house when it was open to the public, and told her about the type of properties his firm handled, and in return Frances filled in a little of her background at York University and her brief spell with the Napiers. A little after ten she rose to go, conscious that her host was beginning to look decidedly weary and dark under the eyes.

'It's early yet, Frances,' he protested politely.

'Nevertheless I think I'd better be on my way. I don't

want to keep Mr and Mrs Bates from their bed—or you. I gather you make an early start in the mornings.'

He grimaced. 'Necessary evil, I'm afraid. Sometimes when my alarm jerks me out of bed on these cold, dark mornings I yearn for a hot, deserted beach in the sun, with nothing to do but lie on it all day. It's the sybarite in me, I suppose.'

'A pleasant thought,' agreed Frances, and went with him through the great hall and into the smaller entrance hall beyond it. 'Goodnight, then Mr—Harry. I'll see you tomorrow evening and make a report on my finds.'

He opened the big door and held it for her. 'I'll see you safely inside the gatehouse, Frances Wilding. I need a word with Bates, anyway.'

Their feet crunched on the gravel as they went across the inner court, which looked almost unreal as fog wreathed the iron sconces which housed the outside lamps. Trails of the thick white vapour hung in the still, cold air and Frances shivered a little, hugging her arms across her chest. Harry put a hand under her elbow and ran with her to the gatehouse, hammering on the door for admittance. Mrs Bates threw it open, clucking in disapproval at Frances's coatless state, and shooed her upstairs as Harry said goodnight and went into the parlour to talk to Bates.

'You get undressed and pop into bed.' Mrs Bates smiled kindly and went downstairs, leaving Frances to hurry through her preparations for the night as obediently as if she were one of Mrs Bates's former charges, thinking it was small wonder Harry Curthoys still jumped to obey when his old nurse commanded it, even if he was lord of the manor and all that.

She put out the light and stretched luxuriously in the comfortable bed, thinking of Chris who had always known where he was going and what he wanted to do—no waffling about for him. He intended to be successful and make money, and no doubt would, which was just as well, as his future wife was never likely to earn much. Their only arguments had been over her choice of career. Chris had wanted her to do something likely to bring in more money, but Matt Wilding, having known him since childhood, made it clear in no uncertain terms that his daughter was free to come to her own decisions. Frances smiled at the memory and curled up ready for sleep, warmed by the thought that Christmas was only a few weeks away and she would soon be seeing Chris again.

Next morning she was up early, already dressed for work when Mrs Bates tapped at the door with her breakfast tray.

'You mustn't run after me with trays!' Frances protested. 'I can come downstairs and fetch it—or, better still, eat breakfast down there with you.'

'Certainly not, Miss Frances.' Mrs Bates looked shocked. 'It's no trouble. Just leave it by your bed when you've finished and Bates will collect it later after he's seen to the fires over at the Court. I must get over there myself now—I have help in from the village on Mondays. Come and see me in the kitchen when you're ready to make a start and I'll give you the keys to the attics.'

Frances had finished her breakfast, tidied her room and made her bed long before eight-thirty. Ready for the day in jeans and warm sweater under a fisherman's canvas smock, she took her tray downstairs and, not bothering with a coat, ran across the inner court and went into the house. She made her way to the kitchen, knocked on the door and went in to find Mrs Bates cooking on the outsize electric stove, her husband feeding the Aga with fuel and Harry Curthoys sitting on one end of the huge, scrubbed-top table, swinging his legs and drinking orange juice.

'Good morning.' Harry jumped down from the table, smiling, and held out a chair for her. 'You're an early bird, Frances. You're not due to start until nine, you know.'

'I just came to get the keys. I thought you'd have gone, Mr Curthoys.'

He frowned blackly at her at the formality, and sat down beside her to demolish the plate of bacon, eggs and mushrooms that Mrs Bates set before him.

'I'm off to look at a house in Sutton Hardacre this morning. The appointment was made originally for eleven o'clock, but the chap rang up at the crack of dawn and asked if I could get there by nine-thirty so there's no point in going to the office first. I must ring my secretary and tell her of the change of plan. Good thing, really, I'll have time to see you started before I go.'

The Bateses left them, to start on the chores of the day, and Harry offered Frances some toast when they were alone.

'No, thanks. I'd already eaten quite a lot before I came over.'

'Not enough to suit Dolly. You've made quite a hit with her, by the way,' he added. 'She thinks you're a very nice-mannered young lady, not pushy and covered with make-up like some she could mention.'

Frances gave a husky little giggle. 'I sound excessively dull!'

'I wouldn't say that,' said Harry cheerfully and jumped to his feet, going to a rack that held a row of large iron keys. 'They're all labelled, Frances, should you need any of them. Here is the bunch for the attic rooms, so if you're ready we'll go up.' He collected a powerful torch from a shelf and led the way from the room, turning immediately up a narrow flight of stairs Frances hadn't noticed before. 'The back stairs, which are a bit steep,' cautioned Harry. 'So watch your step.'

'I suppose this was the route the hot water travelled in pre-bathroom days,' commented Frances.

Harry paused as they reached the narrow spiral leading to the attics. 'Seriously, Frances, if you do need anything brought up here or taken down, ask me or Bates or anyone who's around. Please don't attempt it yourself.'

'I'm stronger than I look!'

'Possibly, but I don't want you breaking your neck while juggling with a trunk full of Curthoys household accounts, so please leave the strong-arm bit to the rest of us.' His face was serious, and Frances nodded gravely in response.

'OK. I'm really quite sensible.'

'It must be hard convincing people of that, when you look so much like a pet kitten!'

Frances stared at him, open-mouthed, and Harry Curthoys laughed indulgently.

'Hasn't anyone ever told you that before?'

'No.' She looked away, embarrassed. 'Perhaps you could open up now, so I can get on.'

He unlocked the attic door promptly, peering into her face in contrition. 'Oh, Lord, now I've put my foot in it again, haven't I?'

Frances made no answer as she preceded him into the dusty, cluttered room, her fleeting annoyance banished instantly by the smell of paper and ink and old leather. Her nostrils flared slightly with anticipation, and she drew in a deep breath of satisfaction as she became suddenly businesslike.

'If you could just put the torch on that cupboard over there, I'll clear this table to work on, and do you think I could have a kitchen chair of some kind——'

'You can have anything you want,' Harry said instantly, 'but I thought the idea was to bring some of this stuff down to work on in the library?'

'I'll be just fine—really.' Already Frances's attention was elsewhere as she began to clear the table. Harry watched her in wry amusement for a moment, then went to the door.

'I'll leave you to it, then. Shout for Bates if you need anything.'

'What? Oh, yes, I will—thanks,' said Frances absently, and plunged back into her perusal of a bundle of ancient, mouse-nibbled household accounts, not even noticing when her new employer shrugged philosophically and left her to the potent fascination of the past.

Frances worked steadily all morning, only surfacing momentarily to drink the coffee Bates brought her at eleven. She was quite taken aback when Mrs Bates came up to the attic promptly at one to say that lunch was ready in the library, where Miss Frances was to work for the rest of the afternoon as Mr Harry had instructed.

'Oh, but Mrs Bates, couldn't I just finish this bit——'

'No indeed, Miss Frances. For one thing you'll catch your death of cold up here. Just look at your hands—quite blue they are.' From the look on her face Mrs Bates was in no mood to be gainsaid. 'You just tell me what you want carried down and Bates can see to it. Then you can work in the library, where it's warm. Bates has a nice fire going in there.'

'But everything's so dusty, Mrs Bates—I can't possibly work on that beautiful table,' protested Frances as she meekly followed the stout figure down the stairs.

'I'll put some holland covers on it. You can spread them over the carpet too, if you like,' panted Mrs Bates, and gave Frances a smile of approval as they reached the back hall. 'Though I'm very pleased to see you're so thoughtful about such things.'

After a much-needed wash, Frances settled at the now-shrouded library table, warmed by the leaping flames of a log fire as she enjoyed creamy leek and potato soup and a slice of hot mushroom tart for lunch. Afterwards Bates carried in the chest Frances had requested be brought down for her afternoon's work.

'I must apologise, Miss Frances,' he said breathlessly. 'I'm afraid I let the chest slip on the back stairs—missed my footing on the bend.'

Frances jumped to her feet in concern. 'Did you hurt yourself?'

'No, no, miss.' He examined the chest anxiously. 'The lid's taken a bad knock. I fancy there's something heavy inside, a metal box of some kind.'

Frances went down on her knees and opened the chest with care, finding that the false wooden lining of the lid had been splintered by contact with an old deed-box crammed down on the ledgers and papers beneath it.

'Not too much harm done, I think. Everything's very neatly packed in here. I shall spend a very interesting afternoon going through this lot.' She ran a hand lovingly over the chest, which was a very plain wooden affair, sturdy, but hardly an item of luggage she would have expected a Curthoys to own. The initials L M were carved on the lid, and Frances eyed them speculatively, curious as to their origin.

Bates watched her indulgently. 'You look as though you're enjoying yourself, Miss Frances,' he observed.

'I am,' she assured him, 'thoroughly! The contents of this particular chest are in the best condition of the lot, apart from the contemporary records. Someone in the mid-seventeenth century made a very meticulous chronicle of life at Curthoys Court right up to the time of the Restoration, from just a cursory glance through.' She looked at him hesitantly. 'Forgive my curiosity, but have you been here long?'

'Most of my life, Miss Frances, except for a spell in the army at the back end of the war. My father was butler to Mr Harry's father, and I became his replacement when he died. Before that I'd been footman and helped out generally under my father's eye—and a right old Tartar he was, too. Harder on me than the rest of the staff, but I daresay it did me no harm.'

'So you were here when Mr Curthoys was born?'

'Yes, miss. He and Miss Charlotte spent a lot of time in the kitchen and the stables when my wife—who was their nanny then—turned a blind eye. Old Mr Curthoys disapproved, but Miss Nadine, Mr Harry's mother, only laughed and told me not to let them be nuisances.' Bates smiled reminiscently, then recollected himself. 'But I'm keeping you from your work, Miss Frances. My wife will bring you tea later on.'

Frances would have liked to hear a lot more about the childhood of Harry Curthoys, but forgot him almost at once as she delved into her treasure trove, which was what the contents of the trunk proved to be. There were ledgers, leatherbound, with pages yellowed and dog-eared by time, some of the ink very faded but most of the entries still

legible. Then came miscellaneous deeds, neatly rolled and
tied, manorial records, estate books, game books, garden
books, household accounts, estimates, plans, the list was
endless. It was all there, a painstakingly documented
account of a period of great turbulence in the Curthoys
family history.

Eyes glistening, Frances took everything out carefully,
putting it into date order as she went, until the chest was
empty. She would never have known that the chest
contained something else if Bates hadn't fallen and
damaged it as a result, something that would have
remained hidden behind the false lid which had splintered
and broken to reveal a glimpse of reddish leather, soft as silk
to the touch. Frances gently drew a slim book from its
hiding place. Taut with expectation she opened it, her
mouth drying with excitement as she read the words,
Arabella Curthoys. Her Journal. 1646.

Here were riches indeed. This must be the diary written
by the wife of the mysterious, fascinating Hal Curthoys,
who had lain down on a summer's day and died at the very
time he was restored to his wife and family after fighting for
his king. Frances itched to fall on the book and devour its
contents, but some scruple held her back. She felt strongly
that Harry Curthoys should see it first, give her the go-
ahead. Which was probably silly under the circumstances—she was being paid to go through everything.
Nevertheless this slender volume of such powerful allure
was different. She laid it to one side, and applied herself to
the other contents of the chest.

It was all so absorbing, and presented such a clearly
depicted portrayal of life under Charles Stuart, that
Frances came back to the present with an effort when Mrs
Bates came in with a tea tray and told her to wash her hands
with all the brisk kindness once employed with young
Harry Curthoys and his sister Charlotte.

She told Harry about the book while they were eating later
that evening.

'A diary!' Harry leaned forward and whistled, his meal forgotten. 'Whose?'

'Arabella Curthoys,' said Frances in triumph.

'Hal's wife!' He sat back, and surveyed her with eyes narrowed to gleaming slits. 'And what does the fair Arabella have to say?'

'I don't know yet. I thought you'd prefer to look at the diary first.'

'Why?' asked Harry blankly.

Frances shrugged, embarrassed. 'It seemed such a personal thing to read—particularly when it's been hidden all this time. Deeds and household accounts are one thing, but I thought you might not like me to read anything as private as a diary until you've had a look at it first.'

'My dear girl, you have *carte blanche* to read anything you like,' he assured her, 'but since you've been so good-mannered we'll take a look at the diary together. You never know, it may shed some light on the mystery of Hal Curthoys's death.'

CHAPTER THREE

FRANCES had carefully dusted the slim leather book when she found it, and now, as she handed it to Harry, she was conscious again of the same feeling of reluctance experienced earlier. To read the writer's private confidences seemed such an intrusion, even though the lady had been dead for well over three hundred years.

Harry's face fell as he eagerly opened the book to the first page, and he stared in frustration at the ornate, faded script.

'Hell's bells, how is one supposed to decipher this lot? Look at all these fancy curlicues, and the letter "s" written as "f" in some places!' He turned rueful eyes on Frances. Eyes, she realised, that were not dark brown as she had thought but very dark grey, like pewter, now they were seen at close quarters. 'Well?' he demanded, and she jumped.

'I'm sorry.' She flushed. 'What did you say?'

'I said you'll have to read aloud to me if I'm going to understand it,' he said patiently. 'Where were you for a moment? Back in the seventeenth century?'

'Yes,' lied Frances hastily, and turned her attention to the journal, which at first appeared to be a fairly uneventful account of daily life at Curthoys Court at the time, with mentions of the husband who was expected home soon from Oxford.

'Hal sends word,' wrote Arabella, 'that he has compounded for the estate. By this means he may purchase both peace and pardon with one single payment according to the value of our lands.'

'I knew he did that, of course,' said Harry. 'All but beggared himself to do it when Cromwell ordered the King out of Oxford. The house had already been sequestered,

40

anyway—stripped to the bone by the Roundheads. All the ornaments and tapestries and more portable furniture were taken. Most of what's here now dates from the Restoration onwards.'

'Must have been awful for poor Arabella, left alone to cope with all that,' said Frances with feeling.

'There'd have been some servants left, of course, but otherwise Arabella was singularly alone in the place for that period. Hal's father and two younger brothers were killed at Edgehill, and his mother only survived them by weeks. Anyway, that's ancient history, Frances, let's see if she tells us anything new.'

'My little Ned has been sick this fortnight,' wrote Arabella, 'but is now recovered and makes much noise again.'

Harry grinned. 'Nothing changes, does it?'

'At noon,' went on Arabella, 'I must set out for Astcote. I shall not send L., I must see him myself, warn him of Hal's return. Dear God, how shall I bear it——'

There was no further entry for that day, nor for the several days afterwards. Then came more commonplace references to household routine, but then, in an unsteady, smudged hand:

'Hal is come home. Little Ned and all of Curthoys Court rejoices.'

'Except, it would seem, the fair Arabella,' said Harry, and turned a cynical look on Frances. 'Are you getting the same vibes from this diary? Do you agree that Hal came home to something less than a rapturous reception from his wife?'

Frances nodded thoughtfully.

'This man she had to warn. Could it have been a lover?'

'Very probably. Perhaps Arabella found her chastity hard to bear in Hal's absence.' Harry's face looked bleak. 'Women can be changeable creatures. Maybe she found a Roundhead more to her taste while her Royalist was away.'

Frances made no comment, and went on poring over Arabella's script, which grew less legible as page succeeded page. Some were blank, others held only references to routine matters. Then came a date in June, when Arabella had written:

'Hal is bitter, changed. He sleeps no more in my bed. I cannot be sorry. How can I, when it is not my lawful husband I desire at my side, but only he who is forbidden to me.'

Then more trivia followed before another, impassioned entry.

'I know Hal to be angry, wounded in his heart and in his manly pride. Sometimes I fear what he will do. But I cannot, I cannot. Life is insupportable. I desire only one man's touch. I am sick with longing. Sweet Jesu, how may I bear it——'

Frances drew a deep breath and let it out again slowly. 'Poor woman. She was desperately unhappy.'

'So was Hal, by the sound of it,' retorted Harry. 'Just imagine coming home from the wars to find someone else had been enjoying the privileges he fondly imagined were being saved for himself!'

'And of course Hal would have been scrupulously celibate all that time himself, no doubt,' commented Frances drily.

Harry's face relaxed, 'No. Of course he wouldn't. No one would have expected it of him.'

'Not even Arabella?'

'It seems as though Arabella had other fish to fry.' There was sarcasm in the light, drawling voice.

'From the anguish coming through from these pages her feelings for this other man were more than a mere passing fancy,' said Frances tartly. 'Perhaps she really loved him. After all, her marriage to Hal Curthoys would probably have been one of the usual arranged affairs of the time— maybe she didn't care for him very much.'

'From what she says, though, Hal seems to have cared for her all right. "Wounded in his heart", she says, and she was afraid of what he'd do.'

'Is that why he committed suicide?'

Harry speared her with a bright look of astonishment. 'Why do you think he committed suicide?'

'Because his tomb is railed off in the church. That's what happened sometimes, if the suicide was of good family and above being buried at the crossroads.'

'But it was Arabella who had the railing put up, as far as I know,' said Harry. 'I'm sure you'll find a mention of it in the records somewhere. The tomb attracted so many people the railings were erected against the over-enthusiastic public—officially, at least.'

'Interesting,' commented Frances, and looked uneasily at the open, leatherbound volume in front of her. 'And you've never seen or heard of this book before?'

'Never knew it was in existence. It's probably been stuck in the lid of that chest since the writer hid it there. Though why the silly creature failed to destroy it beats me.'

'Let's see if we can find out. The initials L.M. are on the lid of that chest so it couldn't have been Arabella's—too plebeian for her, anyway.' Frances riffled through the pages. 'There's not a lot more in here. Shall I go on?'

Harry leaned back in his chair comfortably.

'By all means, Scheherazade. It reads like a thriller.'

Hurriedly Frances returned to the ornate handwriting, which grew wilder and less easy to decipher by the page. It was plain that Arabella Curthoys had needed a confidante desperately, and the only one whose discretion she could rely on was her diary. Blots appeared as if she had stabbed the paper with her pen as she scrawled her innermost feelings on the thin pages.

The picture grew clearer. The anonymous lover, unable to bear the thought of his lady available to her husband's embrace, had smuggled a phial of poison to his love, and she, in anguished obedience, had given it to Hal in the jug of ale she took him in the garden as he lay reading in the sun. She had left him to drink it alone, and he had died. But by no means in the graceful pose of the figure on the tomb.

'I forbade Ned or the servants to disturb him, and did return myself later. Not to mine own dying day shall I forget. I straightened his limbs, that were drawn up and twisted in mortal agony, and I turned his face, oh, sweet Jesu, his face that had been so pleasing, until it was hid in the crook of his arm. Only then did I scream and cry for aid and send L. for the doctor. I have paid a terrible price for my love, and can tell only these blank pages of my sin. Soon shall I burn this book, and with it all memory of this blackest day.'

Frances's voice grew huskier than usual with the last few sentences, and there was dead silence in the room when she finished.

After a time Harry shook himself, like someone trying to wake from a bad dream. 'My God,' he breathed. 'Why did Arabella never burn her diary? She can hardly have wanted a load of dynamite like that hanging about for all and sundry to see.'

Frances felt oddly chilled, and rose to go over to the fire, holding out her hands to the blaze. 'Perhaps she gave it to this L.M. whoever it was, for safe keeping.' Something occurred to her. 'Did Arabella ever marry again, by the way?'

'No, she didn't. In fact she died only a year or so after Hal.'

'Did she have any joy of her lover at all then, do you think?'

'I hope not.' Harry gazed at her absently. 'You know, Frances, Arabella probably had Hal's tomb railed off to indicate that his death was suicide in order to kill any suspicions anyone may have felt towards herself.'

Frances shivered. 'So not only did she kill her husband, but she let him die unshriven, and left him with the slur of suicide as well, which was pretty heavy in those days. Not very nice, our Arabella.'

Harry went over to the desk and inspected the contents of a tantalus standing on it. 'Have some brandy, Frances. I could do with one after Arabella's revelations.'

Frances normally disliked brandy, but for once she was grateful for the warmth the spirit gave her. Harry stood beside her by the fire, gazing down into the flames.

'I wonder who this lover of hers was,' he said musingly. 'From all the frantic secrecy do you think the chap was one of Cromwell's lot?'

'Hardly likely, considering they were Puritans and pretty down on sin of any kind, let alone adultery and murder,' Frances pointed out.

'Then he must have been one of the so-called lower orders, a bailiff, even a groom—perhaps you'll find out something when you go through the rest of this stuff.' Harry smiled at her warmly. 'You've made quite a spectacular start, Frances Wilding. If this is the sort of thing you come up with on your first day what are you likely to find as you go on, I wonder?'

Frances sipped her brandy, then shook her head deprecatingly.

'Nothing so riveting, I should think, at least not to you, perhaps. I find it *all* riveting, but not everyone shares my passion for the daily minutiae of the past.'

'That's for sure.' Harry gave a great yawn, and at once Frances put down her empty glass.

'Time I was off,' she said briskly.

Harry made no attempt to detain her, presumably as anxious to get to bed as she was, but to her surprise he led Frances towards the stairs as they left the library.

'Let me show you something before I walk you back,' he said, and beckoned her upwards to the long gallery, which looked rather daunting late at night, despite the lights he switched on as they reached it. He went over to the great stone fireplace half-way along the room and pressed another switch. Several portraits were illumined by the lights suspended above them.

'*Voilà*,' said Harry, and made a dramatic bow to the lady on one side of the fireplace. 'May I introduce you? Miss Wilding, Lady Arabella Curthoys.'

Frances moved forward to gaze up at a woman with the stylised beauty of a typical portrait of the period. Glossy jet-black ringlets threaded with pearls framed a face whose beauty might have been bland, but for the eyes, which were lambent with melancholy. Frances looked at Harry questioningly.

'Was this——?'

'Painted during the period between her marriage and the birth of her son. Not very cheerful, is she?' He took her by the arm and led her to the portrait on the other side of the fireplace, the head and shoulders of a man in his late twenties. Hal Curthoys. There was a lack of ostentation about the painting that appealed to Frances strongly; no silks and satins, just the fine lace of the trimming on the collar of his shirt, one small gold earring in the ear just visible through the fair hair that touched his shoulders. And the face was more than a little like Harry's. Even the watchful, wary expression on the finely cut features was similar, as though life had dealt Hal Curthoys a difficult hand to play too. Which it had, thought Frances in sympathy, a lot worse than Harry's, one way and another.

'So there they are,' she said softly. 'Both of them to die so young.'

'Hal got the raw deal, but for Lady Arabella an early demise was no more than her just deserts, by the sound of it,' he said flippantly.

'*Lady* Arabella?'

'Daughter of an earl. Quite a catch for Hal, who had no title, even if the first Curthoys did come over with William the Conqueror—or so it's always been claimed.' Harry switched off the portrait lights and waved Frances ahead of him as he plunged the gallery into darkness. 'Her rank would have helped protect her, even if anyone had harboured any suspicions. No one would have voiced them about an earl's daughter.'

Frances nodded thoughtfully. 'Above suspicion by birth rather than character. Did the Curthoys line come down unbroken from father to son?' she added, as they went downstairs.

'Lord, no. It swerved all over the place, cousins and second cousins, sprigs of noble houses who changed their names to marry the daughter of the house when there was no son to inherit. But somehow we've managed to survive up to the present day.' Harry helped Frances on with her coat, and gave a dispirited shrug. 'It's from now on that things are likely to get rocky. I'm the only male of my generation. Charlotte, to her sorrow, is unable to have children. So there we are. End of story.'

Frances kept her eyes on the way ahead as their footsteps crunched over the gravel of the inner court. 'But surely you'll marry one day?'

Harry laughed. 'I suspect you're an incredible romantic, Frances. Just be thankful you and this accountant of yours have your own neat little future mapped out.' They had reached the light outside the gatehouse by this time, and the mockery in his eyes was plainly visible. 'I can see you now in your stripped-pine, pseudo-Georgian executive lovenest, with your 2.4 children——'

'You're patronising me,' she cut in, and rang the doorbell.

His face sobered instantly. 'Frances—please——' But Mrs Bates opened the door to them, and he halted, mid-sentence.

'Goodnight, Mr Curthoys,' said Frances quietly, and smiled at her new landlady. 'The meal was lovely again, Mrs Bates. Goodnight.'

Frances went up the narrow stairs, slightly appeased by the dismay on Harry Curthoys's face as she left him, but dampened, nevertheless, by his picture of her future with Chris. He had made it oddly unattractive, and she frowned thoughtfully. Perhaps it was a bad idea to get too accustomed to loftier things like dining at Curthoys Court as a matter of course, as if she were Harry's guest rather than his employee. From now on it might be wiser to keep to her proper place and eat her dinner at the gatehouse each evening.

Smarting a little, she undressed at top speed and stretched out in the welcome warmth of the bed, turning to Chris's photograph for reassurance. Soothed at once by the familiarity of the dark, blunt features, Frances sat up again to reach for her writing pad to tell him about her day, then leaned against her pillows, biting the tip of her ballpoint pen, frowning as she thought about the evening. The revelations of Lady Arabella had dominated it, and without being able to mention that at this stage there seemed surprisingly little to write about. Which was odd. Normally she had no problem in finding something to write about to Chris, however humdrum her day, and today had been anything but humdrum, one way and another. After writing a few lines she gave up. The letter could wait a day or so.

Next morning Frances made a point of being up so early she was downstairs before Mrs Bates could climb upstairs with a tray. Consequently she ate her toast and marmalade at a small table in the window of the parlour, looking out on the moat and rolling parkland beyond while Mrs Bates went over to the Court, to cook Harry's breakfast. It was very pleasant to sit with the morning papers at leisure, knowing she had at least an hour before starting her day's work. She was on her second cup of tea and deep in the book reviews when a loud knock on the door interrupted her and Harry Curthoys strolled in, dressed for the day in a formal suit, the sartorial effect somewhat marred by the muddy rubber boots worn with it.

'Good morning,' he said warily, and smiled. 'Going for a run?'

'No fear! Good morning, Mr Curthoys.' Frances smiled serenely. 'The track suit is strictly for insulation purposes in the attic.'

'Which is why I'm here,' he said at once. 'I've asked a chap to come along today to fix up a light-cluster for you up there, and I'll bring home one of those portable gas heaters with me tonight. In the mean time stay by the fire in the library and content yourself with the records from the chest.'

'Why, thank you. It's very kind of you to go to so much trouble.'

'Nonsense. Not much point in hiring an archivist if I let her freeze to death in the attic!'

Frances got up, eyeing his rubber boots curiously. 'Are you expecting mud on your travels today?'

'I'm just taking a look at the fir trees on the north boundary before I start work. We supply Christmas trees—and holly and mistletoe to the neighbourhood to bring in a spot more income to the estate.' Harry paused, and leaned in the doorway, looking at her quizzically. 'I see I've been relegated to Mr Curthoys since my remarks about your future last night. I didn't mean to be offensive, I was just envious.'

'Envious?' Frances raised an eyebrow.

'Yes.' He pushed himself away from the door. 'So tidy and well organised. No millstone like this place hanging round your necks.'

'But you love your home!'

'True. But the place drains all my resources all the time just to keep it ticking over, without all the repairs and improvements I'd like to make.' Harry sighed and ran a hand through his hair. 'Sorry to bore on about it like this, must be damned off-putting. Anyway, am I Harry again, now, please?'

Frances looked non-committal. 'Frankly I think it might be better to keep things on a more formal footing. I could eat my meals over here in the evenings——'

'Why?' he cut in. The grey eyes were suddenly ice-cold. 'Are you afraid I might get ideas on the *droit de seigneur* line? Lust after your nubile young body?'

Her chin went up. 'That hadn't even entered my head. I merely thought that since you are my employer it would be more fitting——'

'Fitting?' There was a wealth of bitterness in his voice. 'Just say point blank you'd prefer eating alone. You needn't wrap up a disinclination for my company in fancy terminology.'

Dismayed, Frances made an awkward little gesture of apology. 'That wasn't what I meant at all. I enjoyed eating with you very much indeed. But when you painted your little picture of my future it rather brought me up with a jerk, reminded me not to get too used to dining at the Court as if it were my due, when my real life will be nappies and fish fingers, with the odd *boeuf bourguignon* when we have people in to dinner.' Her eyes appealed for understanding, and Harry's face softened.

'Silly child. Which is what you look like this morning in that gear.' He smiled and turned to go, then as an afterthought, 'Anyway, you're relieved of my company tonight. Rotary dinner in Astcote.'

'That's where *he* must have lived,' said Frances, diverted.

'Who?'

'Arabella's lover.'

'Oh, yes, of course. She had to go to Astcote to warn him Hal was coming back, didn't she?' Harry looked at his watch. 'Blast, I'll have to go. Would you hang on in the library until I get home from the office this evening—I'd like to know how you get on today.'

Frances was thoughful as she lingered by the window, watching as the battered Range Rover disappeared from view down the bends of the driveway. There was a lazy, casual air about Harry Curthoys that was very deceptive as to the true nature hidden behind it. The owner of Curthoys Court was a more complex personality than he appeared on first acquaintance: under the friendliness there was a frightening implacability.

A few minutes later she settled herself contentedly at the library table, surrounded by ledgers and account books of every description. Before beginning on them she read through Arabella's journal again with concentration, to see if any further light could be thrown on the dramatic circumstances of Hal Curthoys's death. After she had pored over the pages for some time, nothing new emerged beyond the fact that Ned Curthoys, Hal's young son and heir, was a delicate boy, prone to frequent illness. Frances's eyes narrowed, and she leafed quickly through several pages, more accustomed now to the ornate hand. The child appeared stricken with something or other every few days, as far as she could make out. Admittedly there had been little relief for illnesses then beyond herbal remedies; painkillers were non-existent and the sufferer just had to grin and bear it. And poor little Ned seemed to have suffered more than most.

Abandoning Arabella's confidences, Frances turned to the less dramatic, but no less fascinating entries in the ledgers recording the daily routine of a family living through the balmy days of the King's Peace in the reign of Charles I, right through the Civil War and the sober rule of Cromwell that followed it. She found no mention of anyone who seemed remotely eligible to be my lady's lover.

Frances was so engrossed that she merely smiled vaguely in acknowledgement when Bates brought her mid-morning coffee. He returned to the kitchen to report favourably on the young lady's industry, and Mrs Bates had to shake Frances by the shoulder when she took her her lunch tray later on. Frances stretched and yawned, sniffing the fragrant aroma of piping hot vegetable soup enthusiastically.

'Mm, smells marvellous, Mrs Bates! I had no idea of the time—I'm starving.'

The housekeeper's face took on a carefully casual expression. 'I expect a pretty young thing like you must have lots of boyfriends. Don't they mind you being shut up here?'

Frances shook her head. 'Only one boyfriend, Mrs Bates, and he's just started in his first job in Edinburgh, so we're rather a long way apart to see much of each other at the moment.'

'What does he do then, this boyfriend—that's if you don't mind me asking, of course?'

'Not in the least. He's an accountant.'

'Very respectable,' approved Mrs Bates. 'Mind you, it'll be nice for Mr Harry to have a bit of company for a change. Not much of a life for a young man like him, really, living here on his own.'

'He's got you Mrs B.'

The woman chuckled. 'That's as may be, but he needs a wife of his own, but ever since that Miss Hayward behaved so badly to him I think Mr Harry's off the idea of marriage altogether. Very fond of her, he was. Of course, she had a pretty face, but handsome is as handsome does, I say.'

Frances was seized with an ignoble urge to learn more about the fickle Annabel, but Mrs Bates was already making enquiries about dinner and where her young guest would like to eat it, and after a while went off, leaving Frances to the inventory she was making.

She was still hard at it at six when Harry Curthoys strode into the library and plucked the pen from her hand.

'Hey! When I asked you to wait here until I came home I didn't mean you to work all the time.' He raised his eyebrows at the look of excitement on the face turned up to his. 'What is it? Found some treasure, or something?'

'I think I know who he was,' she answered without preamble, and held out Arabella's journal, which had paper markers interspersed among the pages. 'There—look for yourself.'

Harry took the book, frowning as he flipped through the marked pages. 'What's the big deal? They made preserves here and contrived a new gown from two old ones another day. Slept badly—oh, confound it, Frances, the woman's writing sends me cross-eyed. What exactly *should* I be seeing for myself?'

'You're missing the significance of certain routine items that keep cropping up, Harry. Look——' She came round the desk and leaned over the journal. 'Here's the first, "Ned feverish today." Then a couple of days later "Ned had putrid throat", then "Ned troubled with itching, and so on."

Harry looked sideways with some amusement at her flushed, triumphant face. The short dark curls were standing on end as though her fingers had been raking through them, and a smudge of dirt embellished her small nose. 'All right, cleversticks, what's the answer? Was our fair heroine poisoning her son as well, do you think?'

'No, no,' said Frances impatiently, 'but I think she used his dodgy health as an excuse for frequent visits from young Dr Verney, who replaced his infirm father early on in our little tale. Who would question regular visits by the physician to the local big house, particularly when the heir to the place was plagued by what seems to be a much-publicised sickly constitution?'

Admiration dawned in Harry's eyes. 'Of course! And a doctor would have had access to my lady's chamber at any old time, with no adverse comment from the household, into the bargain.'

'Particularly as Lucy, Araballa's maid, appears to have acted as go-between.' Frances beamed at him. 'Dr Verney must have provided his lady with the poison to put in her lord's ale, and then *he* would have been the one called in to examine Hal's dead body and diagnose death from natural causes—I believe seizure was a word that covered a multitude of sins at the time. Neat, wasn't it? There would have been no query about Hal's sudden demise, which would probably have been attributed to the privations of his efforts, fighting for his king, and the subsequent joy and excitement of his reunion with his wife and son.'

Harry clapped vigorously. 'Bravo, Frances. I think you've cracked it!'

'It's only supposition, Harry,' she warned. 'But from the entries in Pegler's ledgers——'

'Pegler?'

'The steward. You can see the payments made regularly to "young Dr Verney" as he was called——'

'You mean the lover was getting paid in *money* as well!'

Frances smiled widely, then sobered. 'But not for long. He hanged himself some time after Hal's death. There's an entry to the effect, because Pegler noted the new doctor's name and made a passing comment on the unfortunate circumstances of young Dr Verney having taken his own life, "to his father's great sorrow".'

Harry whistled. 'Why do you think? Conscience?'

'How about blackmail? The maid, Lucy, was the one who knew everything, so she's the likeliest candidate. She must have found the diary and hidden it, then demanded money from the doctor, and possibly Lady Arabella as well.'

'My God, it beats one of those Jacobean melodramas,' said Harry, and went over to the desk. 'Here—have a sherry. You deserve one.'

'I thought you were going out.'

'I am, but I can spare a moment to toast my erudite little sleuth.' He raised his glass to her. 'Your health, Frances Wilding.'

Frances smiled absently and sipped the sherry, then glanced up at him. 'This is sheer supposition, you know, no real proof.'

'But it doesn't half hang together. I'm positive you've hit every nail bang on the head. Arabella was, quite, literally, a true *femme fatale*. Hal died, the doctor died——'

'Oddly enough so did Lucy, not long after Dr Verney. Pegler mentions paying for the coffin for one Lucy Manders who died suddenly of, guess what? A seizure!'

'Did she, by God!' Harry stared at her. 'Do you suppose our Arabella bumped Lucy off too?'

'More than likely if she was blackmailing her mistress, and keeping the diary hidden as a sword to hold over Arabella's head. It must be her chest, Lucy's, I mean, by the initials L.M. on it, and the diary was hidden in the lid.'

'So Arabella died without ever recovering it.' Harry shook his head. 'She must have gone off her rocker, thinking it could turn up any time in the wrong hands.'

'Maybe that's why she died so young.' Frances sighed. 'But that we'll never know. I can't find any reference to Arabella's death beyond the bare fact that it happened. And Ned, it seems, survived.'

'He certainly did. In spite of all the mollycoddling he grew up to be a right old reprobate. Had two wives, eight legal children and a suspicious number of Curthoys lookalikes in the neighbourhood as well.' Harry put down his glass and perched on the desk, one leg swinging idly. 'Are we back on informal terms then, Frances? I think I heard you say Harry there when you weren't thinking.'

Frances made no reply, suddenly conscious of her dirty hands and generally rumpled state.

'Now you've gone all shy on me,' observed Harry, and smiled cajolingly. 'Why do you object to an informal relationship?'

'I told you. You're my employer——'

'Oh, not all that again! Keep it to Harry—please? And you'll only be called upon to dine with me two or three times a week, I promise. Is that such a hardship?' His eyes danced wickedly, and Frances came to the conclusion that it would be no hardship at all, quite the reverse. In fact she was fairly sure she would be much envied by most girls of her acquaintance. *And* Harry's.

'No,' she agreed, giving in. 'No hardship at all.'

'Good.' He stood up, stretching. 'I'd better have a bath and get out the old black tie. Formal do tonight. But let me walk you across to the gatehouse first.'

'No, really.' Frances sat down at the desk again. 'I'd like to leave things a little tidier first, then I'll run across on my own. I can hardly come to harm in your own courtyard, and I'm not frightened of the dark.'

Harry gave her a friendly smile as he strolled to the door. 'Independent lady. See you tomorrow, then.'

Frances nodded, smiling, and returned to her papers. It had been a very fruitful day, she thought with a satisfied sigh—and a very busy one. An evening on her own would be quite welcome. Not that dinner with Harry Curthoys would have been an unpleasant prospect because he really was a very friendly, charming man, and she could thank her lucky stars that he had given her the job.

After the exciting revelations of the first day or two, Frances buckled down to the less dramatic attractions of the records intended for display first; the period of the Civil War which was the best documented and in better condition than any others prior to their modern counter-parts. She spent her days very happily, completely absorbed in her work, and the evenings were just as pleasant, whether she dined with Harry Curthoys at the Court or from a tray in her room while she read or watched the portable television brought with her from home.

Once Frances had reassured her father that she was perfectly happy at Curthoys Court she stayed there without a break, except for the occasional trip to Astcote or Oxford to do a little shopping. It was only a short time to Christmas, and Frances was looking forward to it impatiently, eager to see Chris again and tell him all the things she found so hard to write in her letters. It was one thing to murmur breathless private things in the actual heat of his embrace, but to write them down in cold blood on paper was quite beyond her.

Harry Curthoys handed over a month's salary on December 1st, brushing aside her protests about having worked only part of November.

'You'll need it for Christmas presents,' he said. 'Regard it as a little bonus for your discoveries about Arabella. God knows, it's not all that much.'

Frances was grateful and assured him that added to her bed and board her salary was perfectly adequate, and went off to shop carefully for Christmas gifts the following weekend. There was an ancient Morris Minor estate car in the stables, and to her delight, Harry insisted she borrow it whenever she wished, as long as she treated the old car with respect.

Her life was so busy and her work so interesting, Frances hardly noticed at first when Chris's letters grew less frequent, and even when she did she was unperturbed. There had been many periods in their long relationship when communication broke down, mainly at exam times, and Frances assumed Chris was finding life demanding in the big outside world, particularly as he was going on with more studies some evenings in his determination to forge ahead with his career. He wrote that he was pleased she

liked her job, hoped her employer was kind to her, advised
her not to get too wrapped up in her mouldy old archives,
and he was looking forward to seeing her at Christmas,
though he would only be home for a day or two since he had
to get back to work before Hogmanay. Reading between
the lines Frances smiled, fairly sure Chris had something
lively lined up for his first Scottish New Year's Eve. His
letters were similar to her own, chatty accounts of his daily
life, with no searing words of love, not by any stretch of the
imagination the type of epistles to sigh over and tie up with
pink ribbon.

On the Sunday before Christmas, Harry took Frances for
a walk to the section of the estate devoted to the fir trees sold
to the public. She watched, fascinated, as families made
their choices and noisy pink-cheeked children swarmed
everywhere, already infected with pre-Christmas excitement. Since trade was so brisk Harry immediately pitched
in and lent a hand. The day was crisp with frost and very
bright, and customers had come out in droves. Not only for
the trees but for the holly and mistletoe on sale.

'Nothing like utilising our natural resources,' Harry said
in an aside to Frances.

'Can I help, please?' she asked eagerly, noticing that
Mason, the gardener, and his two assistants were run off
their feet.

'OK, yes. You take the money for us, then.' Without
waiting for an answer, Harry turned away to organise a
new routine, leaving the elderly Mason and one of the lads
in charge of the packing, while he helped the other boy to
carry the trees and stow them in car boots and on roof racks.
Frances was utterly fascinated by the trumpet-shaped
metal tube into which the boy pushed the tree, trunk first,
so that it emerged to Mason at the other end neatly encased
in polythene wrapping. Not that she had much time to
watch after the first minute or two. The money came in
swiftly and she was kept busy with tying up great bunches
of holly and mistletoe briskly, laughing with the customers,
when the same jokes kept recurring about free kisses from

the saleslady even from respectable fathers surrounded by their young. Despite the cold she soon grew very warm and abandoned her sheepskin jacket and worked, like Harry and the others, in sweater and trousers, her feet warm in thick socks and rubber boots. She had crammed a scarlet woollen cap over her curls to match the sweater Jassy had given her, and received several good-natured compliments from customers who told her she looked like the spirit of Christmas.

'More like a little robin, in my opinion,' observed Harry, when the morning rush was over. He helped her into her coat and laughed at her flushed, bright-eyed face. 'Quite a saleslady you turned out to be, Frances.'

'I enjoyed myself enormously this morning,' said Frances as they went at a brisk pace through frost-rimed fields in the direction of the Court. 'Thank you for letting me come.'

'I should be thanking *you*,' Harry retorted, 'or paying you overtime, at least. When do you want to leave for home, by the way?'

'Is the day before Christmas Eve all right? Chris is coming home then.'

'Who am I to keep you from your lover? Go sooner if you wish.'

'No. The twenty-third will be fine.'

'Right. Stay over New Year, I'll be away at Charlotte's for Christmas, and I gather Bates's niece is coming to spend a day or two over the holiday with them at the gatehouse.'

'Yes. Mrs Bates asked me if I'd mind her sleeping in my bedroom, which was very nice of her. It's *her* spare bedroom, after all.'

'Mine, actually,' said Harry without emphasis. 'And if you'd prefer it kept for your sole use they can all move over into the Court for Christmas.'

Frances stared at him, horrified. 'Heavens, no! I'll just take all my things when Dad comes to collect me——'

'You can borrow the Morris, if you like. Save your father a trip, and you can use it to run about in at home.'

Frances hardly knew what to say. 'I really don't know—

you're much too kind——'

'Drivel,' he said cheerfully. 'I won't need it. Take it.'

On impulse Frances stretched up to kiss his cheek, which was icy cold to her lips, then jumped away again quickly, embarrassed as he grinned from ear to ear.

'If that's the response to a clapped-out old Morris, what would you do if I could lend you a Porsche?'

'Refuse,' she said promptly, and laid a theatrical hand on her heart. 'I am not to be tempted by such lures, kind sir.'

Harry twirled an imaginary moustache and took the hand in his to kiss it. 'Ah. Fair maiden——' He broke off in consternation as he saw her hand, which was criss-crossed with fine cuts and smears of dried blood. 'Good God, how did you do that?'

'Holly.'

'Then come on, let's run for it and get you scrubbed with antiseptic or something, Dolly'll have my head if you get an infection.'

'Don't fuss,' panted Frances as he hauled her across the stable yard at top speed. 'My tetanus shots are up to date and I never get infections.'

'And you're not going to start now, if I can help it.' He pushed her through the door into the big kitchen, where Mrs Bates was stirring something on the Aga.

'Mr Harry! Wherever have you been?' she began militantly. 'This risotto is just about ruined!'

'Never mind that, Dolly. Where's the first-aid box?'

Lunch was forgotten as Mrs Bates exclaimed at the two small scratched hands Frances was made to hold out for inspection. In a very short time the wounds were bathed and anointed, and the risotto served at the kitchen table to save time, which arrangement met opposition from Mrs Bates at first, though she thawed when she heard how good the Christmas tree trade had been.

'Took quite a bit of cash, Dolly darling,' said Harry with relish. 'Every little helps.'

After lunch, Frances retired to the gatehouse for a bath and a lazy time on her bed with a book before beginning to wrap the Christmas gifts bought a few days previously in Oxford. There was a box of cigars for Bates and a porcelain pot filled with hyacinths for Mrs Bates, both of which had been relatively easy. Harry's gift presented a problem. It had been difficult to think of a suitable present for a man who was a contradiction in terms, simultaneously hard up and yet possessor of more beautiful things than most. In the end Frances had opted for the inexpensive and frivolous and bought a checked yellow Rupert Bear scarf in soft wool. She looked at it, hoping he wouldn't think her mad, and wrapped it hurriedly in shiny, holly-sprigged paper before she could change her mind, writing 'from Frances' on the label with a decisive flourish.

Later, over dinner in the morning-room, Arabella cropped up again in conversation—as she had rather a habit of doing.

'Such a damned shame I can't make use of what you found, Frances,' Harry said, sighing. 'But I can't say I'm keen to publish facts of such lurid variety about my family, even if they are three hundred years old.'

'And they're not facts,' Frances reminded him, 'just supposition on my part. We can't prove anything beyond the fact that Arabella actually killed Hal, and I don't imagine you're keen to publicise that.'

'You're dead right. There was enough uproar over Hal last time. I don't want any more sensation seekers begging to spend the night in the church.' His lips curled in distaste. 'Anyway, they'd be disappointed if they expected Hal to wake up and take a stroll. The poor old lad was poisoned. No romantic rubbish about falling asleep on a summer's afternoon. His dear lady wife did him in good and proper, didn't she?'

'From the records it's obvious she commissioned the tomb with almost indecent haste—probably desperate to foster the picture of the sleeping figure in the public mind locally.' Frances gave Harry some syllabub, then served herself. 'Oh, and yesterday I came across an entry in the admirable Pegler's books——'

'Yesterday?' Harry looked up sharply. 'Why the blazes were you working on Saturday? You're not supposed to work at weekends.'

'I don't see why not if I've nothing else to do.' Her chin tilted defensively. 'You were out for the day so I just carried on.'

'You'll be too tired to enjoy Christmas!'

'No, I won't. I love what I'm doing, and besides, there's such masses of it to go through. But——' She hesitated, a slight flush mounting beneath her clear olive skin.

'But?' he prompted.

'Well, the—the longer I work the more you'll have to pay me,' she blurted.

'Good God, I'm not *that* hard up, Frances!' He shook his head reprovingly and held out his dish for a second helping of pudding. 'My firm is very successful, I'd have you know. In fact, if it weren't for this white elephant of mine I'd be very nicely off, thank you.'

'Have you ever thought of selling it, or giving it to the National Trust?' The moment the words were out Frances regretted them, as Harry's face took on an expression as unfamiliar as it was forbidding.

'This is my home, Frances.' The lazy drawl was gone and he spoke with clipped emphasis. 'While I have any breath left in my body, or a penny to my name, the place stays Curthoys property, every stick and stone of it.'

An awkward silence followed his statement, and Frances began stacking plates on the trolley, feeling very much like a new recruit hauled over the coals by a superior officer.

'I'm sorry,' she said quietly without looking at Harry. 'It's none of my business, of course.'

Harry relaxed at once. 'I didn't mean to bark at you, Frances. You only said what all my friends have said, *ad nauseum*, many times before. It's just that somehow or other, since I've had to go out and slog to keep the place, it's come to mean more to me than it ever did before when I took everything for granted.'

Frances tried to conceal her deep breath of relief, utterly

taken by surprise at the depth of her dismay at Harry's displeasure. 'I can understand that only too well, even after being here myself for such a short time. It's such a harmonious house.'

Harry nodded. 'The only room in the entire place I don't care for is the master bedroom. It's always seemed such a gloomy old room to me, and my mother wouldn't sleep there either, no matter how much my father tried to persuade her, apparently.'

'Is it where Arabella would have slept?'

'I don't really know—probably.'

'Perhaps some of her anguish and guilt and so on was powerful enough to leave traces of her feelings behind——' Frances broke off, smiling sheepishly at the look on Harry's face. 'You think I'm talking nonsense.'

He shrugged. 'Not really. I'd have been very sceptical at one time before reading that damned journal, but now, after all that passion and grief coming across so loud and clear over the centuries—well, let's say I'll keep an open mind.' Harry yawned suddenly, and apologised. 'Must have been all that fresh air this morning.'

Frances rose at once. 'Time for bed, anyway. I'd like to make an early start tomorrow since it's my last day for a bit. I've more or less earmarked the stage I hope to reach before I go.'

'Don't overdo it, Frances. The stuff will all be waiting when you get back.'

Harry walked with her to the outer door, which had been constructed in 1423 for the grand sum of thirteen shillings and sevenpence, he told her as an afterthought. Frances ran a hand over the weathered timbers with a little sigh of appreciation, then insisted on walking back by herself, deaf to Harry's protests as she ran across the frosty lamplit courtyard.

As Mrs Bates opened the door to her, Frances glanced across to see Harry's tall slim silhouette still in the doorway of the Court, and raised her hand in response to his wave before going inside the gatehouse. She was still puzzled by his abrupt reaction to her questions; it was as though she had touched some private wound, and suddenly, that mystery mattered more to her than the long-ago murder of Hal Curthoys.

CHAPTER FOUR

THERE were no more dinners tête-à-tête with Harry Curthoys before Christmas. All his time up to the holiday was fully taken up with social engagements, as it had been for the previous week or two. Frances didn't see him at all until the morning of the day she was leaving for home, when he invited her formally to breakfast before he left for his office in Astcote.

'Couldn't let you go off without marking the occasion,' he said, and pulled out a chair at the table in the morning-room. 'Dolly insists you eat a proper breakfast before you make the journey home—and easy does it on the roads. Icy patches, according to the radio.'

Frances found that once she had made a reluctant start on the perfectly prepared food she was actually quite hungry, and even able to carry on a conversation with her host, which would have surprised her nearest and dearest. She was not known for her vivacity first thing in the morning.

'Going straight home?' asked Harry, who was tackling about three times the quantity of food facing his companion.

'No. I'm lunching at the Napiers' to deliver my Christmas present to Sam—a car which transforms itself into a robot when it hits a wall.'

'Sounds fun for Sam, but death on the Napiers' interior decoration!' Harry passed her the toast-rack. 'Perhaps you'll see Eddy Napier while you're there.'

Not, thought Frances, if I see him first. 'Possibly,' she said out loud. 'But I won't stay there too long.'

'As you can't wait to fly to the arms of your lover!'

'Exactly, she agreed serenely. 'It's been quite a time since we saw each other last, so we'll have heaps to talk about.'

Harry shook his head, his eyes gleaming wickedly at her. 'If I were your swain and hadn't seen you for a month or two, conversation would be the last thing on my mind.'

Frances could feel the heat rising in her cheeks, and busied herself with the coffee-pot. 'Chris and I grew up together,' she reminded him. 'We were good friends long before we—we——'

'Ate of the apple?'

'Found we wanted to get married,' she corrected him, and changed the subject by handing over his present. 'Just a little something to wish you a happy Christmas, Harry.'

His face went blank as he took the gaily wrapped package, then his eyes came up to meet hers with a look in them that deepened her colour even more. 'How very sweet of you, Frances. My instinct is to say "you shouldn't have", but I've always considered that a very ungraceful response to someone's generosity, so I'll say thank you very much indeed instead. May I open it now?'

Searing doubt gripped Frances about the suitability of the scarf, and she heartily wished herself miles away as Harry unwrapped it. He tore at the paper as eagerly as a small boy, and lifted out the checked yellow scarf with a crow of such spontaneous delight Frances sagged a little with relief.

'A Rupert Bear scarf—wonderful!' He jumped up from his chair to give her a smacking kiss on the cheek before slinging the scarf round his neck, where it looked very incongruous against the formality of his dark suit. 'I'll wear it always—even in bed.'

'I hope it goes better with your pyjamas than with that suit!'

'It won't clash, anyway—I don't wear any.' His grin was so disarming Frances could only laugh with him, then he looked in dismay at his watch. 'Lord, look at the time—it passes too quickly in your company, Frances Wilding. Hang on a minute, though, must dash upstairs. Wait here.'

Frances drank a second cup of coffee while Harry was away, absurdly pleased that he had so obviously liked the scarf. His reaction had been too genuine for mere good manners, and she smiled as he reappeared in a hurry, carrying a small package, which he handed to her with a graceful little bow.

'Happy Christmas, Frances, and thank you.'

The cube-shaped package was wrapped in glittering gold paper tied with red ribbon, and had a gift-tag in the shape of a robin.

'Reminded me of you,' said Harry with a grin.

Frances undid the ribbons with care, trying not to tear the heavy foil paper as she took the wrappings from a leather box. She gazed at it, hesitating.

'Go on,' he urged. 'It won't bite you—open it.'

Frances obeyed, to find a miniature inside. The small, gold-rimmed oval held a portrait of a youth in his late teens; a youth with long flaxen lovelocks falling over a deep lace collar and russet satin coat. The face was painted in a stiff, stylised manner, but it was instantly recognisable, even though it lacked the world-weary expression of the older man whose portrait hung in the long gallery.

'Hal,' she breathed, and touched the miniature with a loving fingertip. 'Young Hal, before his world fell apart.'

'Painted just before his wedding day, when he was nineteen years old. There are one or two more, actually— miniatures were the snapshots of their day, of course. Someone, probably Arabella, was resourceful enough to bury them, with other items of jewellery and whatever gold they had, in the vegetable plot, before Cromwell's men arrived to take the rest. Don't you like it?'

Frances literally lusted after the miniature, but had grave misgivings about accepting something that was the property of the Curthoys family. 'It's exquisite, Harry, but——'

'I could have given you boring perfume, or whatever, but my instinct told me you'd like this better. Unless I'm much mistaken you have rather a thing about Hal Curthoys, so I'd like you to have this as a keepsake of your time here at the Court.' Harry reached out and laid a hand lightly on her arm. 'Please accept it, Frances. It isn't as if it were an Elizabethan Hilliard, or anything. The artist's unknown, and it's really not of great intrinsic value.'

She hesitated a little longer, then reached up to touch her lips fleetingly to Harry's newly shaved jaw. 'Then thank you. It's quite the most beautiful present I've ever had, and I'll treasure it, always.'

Harry looked delighted as he picked up his briefcase and shrugged himself into his long riding raincoat. 'Great. I'm glad you're pleased.' He threw the yellow scarf over his shoulder with panache. 'There. How do I look?'

'Fantastic! Though it was intended more for walks down to the King's Arms than wearing to the office.'

'Nonsense. Just the thing for the well-dressed estate agent!' He paused in the doorway. 'I've told Bates to see to the oil in the Morris, but it might be wise to check it yourself from time to time while you're away. Have a safe journey and a good Christmas, Frances, and enjoy yourself with your—with your family. See you next year!'

Frances smiled warmly. 'Right. Have a happy time yourself, too, and thank you once again for Hal's miniature. He's so beautiful.'

'I think you're in love with the chap, Frances!'

'No, just very sorry for him. Life wasn't very kind to him, was it?'

'He was probably a drinking, whoring ruffian who got his just deserts!'

Frances clapped her hands over her ears. 'I won't listen— let me keep my illusions, please, Harry!'

'They're quite safe with me,' he said, suddenly sober. 'And now I really must dash. Goodbye, Frances. Take care.'

'And you, Harry. Goodbye.'

When she was alone Frances sat for some minutes, just looking at the miniature. There was a lordly air about the fair youth, that of a man very certain of his place in the world, and the haughty eyes seemed to hold her in complete fascination, until Mrs Bates arrived to break the spell.

An hour or so later, Frances left for home filled with anticipation. She drove first to the Napiers' home to lunch with Caroline and a wildly excited Sam, who tugged Frances with him on a tour of the Christmas decorations in the house, and showed her all the chocolate ornaments on the tree before she was allowed to eat. Caroline was eager to hear about life at Curthoys Court, and very pleased to learn how well Frances was getting on with the job—and with Harry Curthoys. It was quite late before Frances could tear herself away, after an exchange of gifts and a solemn promise to visit Sam again to see what Father Christmas had brought him.

Frances arrived home to a loving welcome from her father and Jassy, and was swept into the warm, familiar house which seemed oddly small now after the grander scale of Curthoys Court. But the Christmas tree was in its usual place in the hall, already surrounded by piles of packages, a wonderful smell of cooking was in the air, and her dark, attractive father looked so happy and relaxed with his beautiful, blonde wife that Frances rejoiced, suddenly aware that it was very, very good to be home.

'How's life with the upper-crust then, Fanny?' teased Matt Wilding.

'Great.' Frances assured him, and gave her new stepmother a kiss. 'No need to ask how life is with you two, one look is enough.'

Jassy smiled happily as they sat down to enjoy a glass of sherry. 'Can't speak for Matt, of course, but from where I am marriage is just wonderful—can't recommend it too highly! Only I wish I didn't have this nagging feeling that I've pushed you out in the cold.'

'Rubbish,' said Frances forcefully, and leaned forward to touch Jassy's hand. 'I've been away from home ever since I started at university, really, and I never expected to stay here once I found a job anyway, so stop imagining you're the wicked stepmother, woman. Now, what's on the programme for the holidays?'

'Jassy's parents arrive tomorrow, otherwise it's situation normal,' said her father, and began to ram tobacco into his pipe. 'Mrs Bradley was in this afternoon, by the way.'

'Oh, yes, is Chris home yet?'

'Tomorrow, apparently. His mother said he couldn't make it today.'

'Some boring function to do with his job,' said Jassy quickly. 'Now do tell all about Curthoys Court, and Harry Curthoys himself—is he as nice as he seemed that first day? Does he fill the place with gorgeous females and have weekly orgies and so on?'

Frances laughed, swallowing her disappointment over Chris, and proceeded to disabuse Jassy of her ideas on life with Harry Curthoys, then gave her father a run-down on the work she was doing. She talked with such animation that Matt Wilding exchanged a relieved look with his wife as his daughter ran upstairs to her room to unpack. Neither of them had relished telling Frances that Chris would be a day late.

'Hardly worth his making the effort to come home at all,' said Jassy crossly as she added the finishing touches to their dinner. 'He arrives tomorrow then leaves at the crack of dawn on the twenty-seventh.'

Matt lounged against a counter-top, watching appreciatively as his graceful wife moved about the kitchen. 'Well, they've known each other since kindergarten—I suppose he expects Frances to take things like that in her stride.'

'Hm.' Jassy scowled as she peered into a steaming saucepan. 'Takes her for granted, in my opinion.'

Alone in her room, Frances felt much the same way. It had been a bit dampening to hear Chris's change of plan at third hand. She shrugged and decided to forget about it. No doubt all would be explained when he did arrive. She appeared so high-spirited during dinner that her father and Jassy were completely reassured, especially as later in the evening Frances received a phone call from an old girlfriend asking her to join a crowd of friends at the local. Frances went off in the Morris and spent a cheerful, rowdy evening catching up on everyone's news, and telling a little about her own new job—which prompted much teasing about village maidens and wicked squires—before the party broke up and she drove home.

Her father and Jassy were waiting for her with rather odd expressions as she went into the sitting-room, and Frances looked from one to the other uneasily as she sat down.

'What's up? I'm not in too late, or something, am I? Is it smacked-wrist time?'

'Of course not.' Matt took hold of Jassy's hand.

Something had happened to Chris. Frances went cold, and her smile was forced on her small, pointed face.

'So?'

Jassy gave her a tremulous smile. 'I'm pregnant, Frances. We're going to have a baby.'

Frances flew at them, trying to embrace them both at once in the wild joy of her relief. 'But that's absolutely wonderful——' She kissed and hugged them then stood back. 'But why on earth didn't you tell me earlier, over dinner, or something?'

'Jassy was afraid you mightn't care for the idea,' said her father, managing to look triumphant and embarrassed at the same time.

'It's fabulous news, Jassy,' said Frances. 'I'm so pleased for you—super Christmas present for Dad! When is it due?'

'June. I'm giving up my job next month.' Jassy smiled radiantly. 'You know, I don't mind in the least. I thought I would, but it seems pending motherhood changes one's outlook along with one's shape. My career can be resumed at some later date if necessary. I've been a working girl for nearly nine years, so it's rather nice to be doing something else instead—something a lot more creative!'

Matt Wilding came back with a bottle of champagne, and all three sat up to the small hours, toasting the impending happy event until Frances could keep her eyes open no more and fell into bed to sleep like a log until mid-morning next day.

All three Wildings slept late, which turned Christmas Eve into a frantic rush of last-minute shopping, wrapping of presents, stuffing the turkey, making mince pies and lunching in the middle of it all on the Chinese take-away young Mrs Wilding fancied so violently that her husband went off immediately to fetch it.

Jassy's parents arrived in the late afternoon, a friendly, energetic pair who insisted on more champagne the moment they heard they were to be grandparents, and it was a convivial party that eventually sat down to a very late dinner. Frances joined in with all the laughter and jokes, but couldn't help glancing at her watch every now and then. When the telephone rang she flew from the table to answer it, shutting the dining-room door on the noise before picking up the receiver.

'Frances? Hi—it's Chris.'

'Hi! Where are you?'

'In a service station somewhere south of Carlisle. I got held up—bit of a do at work, so I'll be late, I'm afraid. I just rang my mother and asked her to pass on the message, but she insisted I ring you myself.'

Thank you, Mrs Bradley, thought Frances, and made an effort to sound unconcerned.

'OK, Chris, thanks for ringing—see you tomorrow.'

'Good girl—knew you wouldn't make a fuss. *Ciao*.'

And *ciao* to you, Chris Bradley, thought Frances, silently fuming. She put the receiver back, took a deep breath, arranged a gay smile on her face and plunged back into the revelry in the dining-room.

'Hey, you lot,' she said cheerfully, 'I hope you've left some wine for me.'

Frances passed an unquiet night, and woke early next morning, rather like the small Frances in the past, who couldn't wait for Christmas Day to begin. She got out of bed, yawning, and went to the window to crane her neck to see if Chris's car was in the Bradleys' drive, and breathed a sigh of relief when she saw it parked in full view. So he was home at last. She relaxed and stretched, anticipation for the day beginning to stir inside her as she looked forward to seeing Chris again. It seemed aeons since their parting. It would be fun just to talk endlessly, hear about his job, tell him about hers, make arrangements for the weekend she was supposed to be spending in Edinburgh soon.

She shivered a little in the cold, and turned to dive back into bed, dislodging something that fell with a little thud to the floor. She switched on her lamp and saw a bright red woollen sock lying on the floor with "Frances" written on it in glitter. A lump rose in her throat as she took the sock back into bed with her. It was packed with thoughtful little gifts; a tortoiseshell propelling pencil, a tiny box of assorted eyeshadows, the mate to the sock, a minuscule, leather-bound copy of Shakespeare's sonnets, a bookmark with her name on it, a lipstick in the muted shade Frances liked best, and in the toe a tangerine, a bright new fifty-pence piece and a chocolate Father Christmas.

Frances sat gazing at the array for some time, her eyes wet as she tried not to think of the contrast between Jassy's thoughtfulness and Chris's cavalier attitude. She gave a loud sniff, then jumped out of bed and dressed quietly, determined to do something useful for Jassy in return. She stole downstairs and made herself a cup of coffee to drink while she prepared all the vegetables for lunch, aware that all the experts said this should be done immediately before cooking, but ignoring them. Today was different. The idea was to prevent Jassy from getting over-tired in the kitchen.

There was no sign of Chris until Frances returned home from church with the others. He was waiting for them on the doorstep, his arms full of parcels and a broad grin on his dark, good-looking face. The grin was a little sheepish as Frances got out of the car, but she made no comment on his tardiness and chattered away happily as they all went indoors to have drinks, check on the turkey, and exchange presents before hearing about Chris's new life in Edinburgh. He sat on the sofa, large and animated next to

Frances as he drank beer and entertained everyone with anecdotes of his life in Edinburgh.

'And how's life among the nobs?' he teased, grinning at Frances. 'Do you fit in well with the rich and aristocratic?'

'Yes, very easily. Only Harry Curthoys is more aristocratic than rich—he works hard for a living.'

This prompted a barrage of questions, not only from Chris but from Jassy's parents, who lived only a few miles from Astcote and were deeply interested in the struggles of the young owner to keep Curthoys Court going. Eventually, Chris shot to his feet.

'My God, is that the time! Mother'll be on the warpath if I'm not back on the dot for the ceremonial carve-up. Thanks for the beer Mr Wilding, see you all later. *Ciao*, Frances.'

He was off before Frances could do more than blink in surprise, and she was hard put to hide her indignation. He might at least have given her the chance to walk to the door with him for a snatched kiss before he went home, she felt, but her mood soon evaporated in the preparations for the meal, and it was late afternoon, feeling over-full and generally anticlimactic, before Frances had time to think. Her father had taken his in-laws for a stroll while Jassy had a rest on her bed, and Frances sat alone in the sitting-room, staring into the fire, aware of an uneasiness she finally had to acknowledge.

Chris was different. Changed. It had been more like a reunion with a big brother than a lover. Even his present to her bore all the hallmarks of something chosen in a hurry with no real thought for her tastes, which he, of all people, should have known only too well. She had searched for an antique map of Warwickshire for Chris, and had it framed for him to hang on the wall of his flat, while his gift to her had been a bottle of a heavy French perfume she disliked, and which had obviously been gift-wrapped in the shop. She sighed heavily, and went off to have a peaceful soak in the bath, taking the historical novel Jassy's mother had given her, in an effort to avoid thinking about Chris for a while.

Later, when the house was full of friends, Chris was the life and soul of the party, organising charades, helping Matt with the drinks and handing round food, quite obviously bent on avoiding a moment alone with Frances. She received far more attention from one of her father's junior colleagues, and assuaged her hurt by flirting with him shamelessly all evening. It was well after midnight before the party broke up, and once again, Chris left quickly with his mother, only pausing to arrange to see Frances the following morning for a drive and drink at the local.

Frances was ready and waiting when Chris tooted on his horn next day, and ran down the drive, determined to behave as though everything was normal.

'You look very nice today,' he said, as they drove off.

'So do you,' she retorted. And he did, in a hand-knitted Aran sweater that made him look ruddier and healthier than ever. 'You definitely don't look as though you spend all your life crouched over columns of figures.'

He laughed heartily. 'I don't. I play rugby and squash, go for a run every day, weather permitting. Must keep fit.'

'How about the social life?'

'Fair,' he said cautiously. 'I go out for a drink with one of the other accountants from the office quite a bit. How about you?'

Frances gave him a thumbnail sketch of life at Curthoys Court, and would have gone on about her interesting work on the family records but for a dampening lack of attention on Chris's part. A glance at his profile sent her spirits plummeting as she saw the absent, rather grim look on his face. Frances trailed into silence as they reached a stretch of road she knew well. A little further on there was a lay-by giving a view of the river Avon winding peacefully through a landscape of fields. Sure enough, Chris drove into it and stopped the car, turning in his seat to look at her. At one time, Frances would have considered this the signal to unfasten her seat belt and fall into his waiting arms, but not today. Chris had brought her here for a purpose, and if she were honest with herself she had a fair idea of what it was— had been expecting it deep down ever since his late arrival home.

'Out with it, Chris,' she said bluntly. 'What's wrong?'

He sighed. 'You guessed something was up, then?'

'I'm not stupid. Shall we say I suspected it, and hoped against hope I was mistaken.' Frances felt vague surprise to hear herself talking so calmly when she was shaking so much inside it was hard to sit still.

'Frances—oh, Lord.' Chris groaned and turned away to stare miserably through the windscreen. 'I suppose I should have said something in my letters, but that seemed a shabby way of doing things. The thing is——'

'You've met someone else.'

He nodded, unable to meet her eyes. 'The accountant I go out with at night is a girl.'

Frances tried to concentrate on the view, willing herself not to cry, to scream, to fly at Chris with her fists, to plead with him to say it wasn't true. This just couldn't be happening, she thought in a frenzy. There had always been Chris. Always. The thought of life without him was insupportable.

'I didn't mean—didn't want to hurt you, Frances. I'm very fond of you, you know that. But with Isla it's different. The moment I laid eyes on her I fell like a ton of bricks. And she felt the same about me, to my amazement, yet she's so clever, so utterly gorgeous, long, chestnut hair, eyes that change from green to blue——'

'I get the picture,' interrupted Frances brusquely, unable to bear any more. 'Don't worry, Chris. You couldn't help falling in love.' My mistake was in thinking you were in love with *me*, she added silently.

'My mother's very embarrassed about it,' went on Chris. 'She was very uncomfortable at your place last night.'

Frances was more concerned with her own feelings at that moment, and had no time to spare for Mrs Bradley's.

'Is—is Isla the reason you were so late getting home?'

He nodded. 'Yes, and the reason why I'm going back later today. We're getting engaged on New Year's Eve,' he said boldly.

The words acted like blows on Frances. 'It's a trifle sudden,' she said faintly. 'You haven't known her long.'

'Long enough to be sure, though. We both knew right from the very beginning.'

She smiled sadly. 'You used to say *we* were too young for anything like that for years yet.'

'I know.' Chris put out a large hand and crushed one of hers. 'But with Isla it's different.'

Frances winced, pretending his grip hurt, and pulled her hand away. 'If you're driving back today you'll need to get away soon. The forecast's not too good.'

'Frances——'

'Start the car, Chris.' She drew in a deep, unsteady breath and stared blindly through the window. 'I—I just want to go home.'

Chris looked at her uncertainly, biting his lip. 'I'm sure you'll find someone else in no time, Frances. You're a great-looking girl. I mean, there must be dozens of blokes who'd be only too keen to step into my shoes at the drop of a hat.'

His clumsy efforts at comfort only lacerated Frances's feelings even more, and she gritted her teeth, refusing to meet his pleading brown eyes. 'Take me home, Chris, please. Now!'

The note of desperation in her voice finally got through to him, and he started the car, but all the way back he went on and on in his attempts to mollify her and justify himself. Frances said nothing at all, trying to block her ears to his explanations and apologies, and jumped out of the car the moment it stopped. She looked Chris straight in the eye and held out her hand.

'Goodbye, then. I'm glad you told me at last, though for the life of me I can't imagine why you didn't come clean sooner.'

'I didn't want to spoil your Christmas,' he muttered,

reddening, and tried to give her a hug, but she pulled away. 'Can't we still be friends then, Frances?'

'Of course.' She gave him a proud little smile. 'But I need a little time to adjust to the idea, that's all. Safe journey back.' She turned away and ran up the drive to the door, then halted and looked back at him. 'I forgot, Chris,' she called. 'Happy New Year.' Even from a distance, Frances could see him wince, and felt a bleak sort of satisfaction. Then she opened the door and went in, putting on a brave smile to face the others.

CHAPTER FIVE

FRANCES, would have given much to go straight back to Curthoys Court, but since that was out of the question she did her best to behave normally and avoid plunging the entire household into gloom once the news was broken to Jassy and her father. Jassy was wildly indignant at first, and Matt Wilding only marginally less so, but when they realised their attitude was only making things worse for Frances they stopped talking about Chris altogether, and took Frances out as much as possible.

Frances, however, quailed at the thought of tagging along with them like the spectre at the feast, and rang Mrs Bates at the Court, asking if it would be terribly inconvenient if her lodger were to take up residence again earlier than expected. Mrs Bates sounded gratifyingly delighted, Mr Harry was still away, her visitor had gone and she and Bates were very quiet on their own, so Miss Frances was very welcome to go back as soon as she liked.

With a sigh of relief Frances packed her bag and bade her father and Jassy farewell, deaf to their worried protests.

'I'll be better on my own for a bit, truly,' she assured them. 'I need to lick my wounds and get myself together, Harry Curthoys is still away so I can get back to work and occupy my mind with the past, which at the moment is rather more attractive than the present.'

Matt Wilding held her close. 'I don't like to think of you alone on New Year's Eve, little one.'

'Much better for me than trying to be jolly at your knees-up, Dad.' Frances smiled gamely. 'And at least I'll avoid running into Mrs Bradley at odd moments. There's a sort of belligerent guilt about her attitude that's rather hard to bear at the moment. It's nobody's fault, after all. These things happen.'

78

'I just wish it hadn't happened to you, that's all,' he said grimly.

As the Morris went on its sedate way she heaved a great sigh of relief, conscious at the same time that she was not only saying goodbye to her family, but to an entire slice of her life. There was a void where once there had always been Chris, rock solid in her background. But now Chris had Isla and Frances was on her own, and it was painful, as if a physical chunk of herself had been torn away to leave a gaping wound. Her whole attitude to life would need rethinking, she thought bleakly; it would be 'I' instead of 'we' in future. The sunshine only served to underline her melancholy, and Frances was relieved when she reached the gates of Curthoys Court. She drove slowly down the bends of the drive, her spirits lifting as the house came into view, welcoming and utterly beautiful in silhouette against the setting sun.

It was very pleasant to receive a warm welcome from the Bateses, to be away from everything that reminded her of Chris as she unpacked in the pretty little bedroom that already had the stamp of her own particular domain. Frances put the photographs of Jassy and Matt and her mother on the dressing-table as before, but the one of Chris had been left at home, along with the unwanted bottle of perfume—which Jassy had been instructed to pass on to the Save the Children committee as a raffle prize at their next coffee morning.

Frances was tired enough to enjoy eating her supper in bed while she watched a film on television and then read her book, and in some odd, unexpected way it was a relief to be able to feel miserable if she wanted to instead of having to put on an act all the time. Mrs Bates came up to the room late at night with a beaker of hot chocolate, lingering to chat a little before she went to bed.

'You look worn out, Miss Frances,' she commented, looking at the girl's pale, tired face. 'Too many late nights, by the look of you. Mr Harry'll be the same. It's always lively at Miss Charlotte's place—I expect he won't be too sorry to get home.'

'When's he due back, Mrs Bates?'

'The second. Opens up the office the day after.' Mrs Bates took the beaker. 'There. Now you get a good night's rest and only get up when you feel like it.'

'I thought I'd start work again tomorrow, Mrs B.'

'Oh, I don't know about that! What will Mr Harry say?'

'He won't know unless we tell him!'

Curthoys Court had central heating which maintained the house at an even temperature most of the time, but Frances was deeply grateful for the roaring fire Bates lit in the library for her to work there next day. During the afternoon it began to snow just as Mrs Bates brought in a tray of tea.

'It won't affect us much, as I always make sure we've plenty of supplies,' she informed Frances. 'Sometimes it's hard to get even as far as the village when the snow keeps up.'

It was oddly cosy working in the library with the leaping firelight and the snowflakes falling thick and fast past the leaded windows, and Frances plunged into her work with deliberate concentration, glad that the painstaking effort required gave her mind no freedom to think of other things. Just after six she tidied the dust-sheeted table a little, leaving everything ready for the next day, placed a guard in front of the fire and switched out the lights just as Bates came to see if she was ready to go back to the gatehouse. He had a waterproof ready to put over her shoulders, since the weather was rapidly deteriorating.

'It's already quite treacherous underfoot,' he warned, and put a hand under her arm as she picked her way across the inner court, gasping as a sudden gust of wind blew a flurry of snow in her face.

'Not very nice,' Frances panted, and stamped her feet free of snow in the passageway outside the gatehouse. The wind howled along it like a banshee, and Frances was glad to get inside to the warmth and cheerful comfort of Mrs Bates's parlour. That lady clucked over her boarder's bedraggled state and brought a towel to dry the damp black curls, which even in the short distance from the house had become plastered to Frances's head. As she rubbed energetically, Frances sniffed at the wonderful aroma coming from the kitchen.

'What a fantastic smell, Mrs B. What is it?'

'Nothing fancy, just my steak and kidney pie with some nice fresh vegetables. Once you've had your bath I'll bring up your tray.'

Frances smiled cajolingly. 'I don't wish to intrude, but could I eat down here with you and your husband, just for tonight? I don't mind the kitchen, and it *is* New Year's Eve.' Suddenly she very much wanted company rather than a solitary meal in her room.

'Why, of course, Miss Frances, with pleasure. A young thing like you should be out at some party, not here on your own.' Mrs Bates became brisk. 'We'll lay the table in here and open up the bottle of wine Bates got in for Christmas and forgot. We'll make it a special occasion, just the three of us—very nice for us to have company to see in the New Year.'

And very pleasant it was. Frances put on the damson-red Benetton sweater dress Jassy had bought her for Christmas, with sheer black stockings and slender-heeled black suede shoes, adding her father's gift of antique pearl ear-drops in honour of the occasion. Mrs Bates exclaimed at the sight of her, saying what a picture she looked, and Frances felt absurdly pleased, particularly when she saw that both Mr and Mrs Bates had also dressed for the occasion, the latter in her good black dress and the former in his best grey suit. The table was laid with the best china, candles, even Christmas crackers, and they sat down to beef soup and steak and kidney pie, wearing absurd paper hats and laughing at the feeble jokes on the mottoes from the crackers. The wine and firelit warmth soon made red flags fly in Frances's cheeks as she ate the homely, delicious food, and she forgot to be miserable for a fair proportion of the evening, particularly when Mrs Bates brought out old snapshot albums after dinner and showed Frances pictures of Mr Harry and Miss Charlotte from cradle to college graduation. The latter's crowning glory was her wedding photograph, which showed her as a tall, fair bride, very like her brother, smiling from a mist of tulle and flowers alongside her tall, burly bridegroom.

'I just wish Mr Harry would follow suit,' sighed Mrs Bates, and urged Frances to more coffee. 'Have a drop of brandy in it, dear, it helps keep out the cold.'

Snow outside or not, Frances was glowing like a rose in her warm dress, and enjoying tales of Harry's childhood, when suddenly all three of them shot to their feet in alarm at the sound of squealing brakes followed by a loud crash outside. Bates ran from the room to investigate. Frances would have followed suit, but Mrs Bates held her back.

'Bates will have taken his shotgun, Miss Frances. I can't let you go out there until we know what it is.'

Both of them stood, tense, then at the sound of voices from the stable yard Mrs Bates relaxed visibly.

'That's Mr Harry,' she said, and patted Frances on the shoulder, telling her to sit by the fire again. 'I don't know what he's doing here tonight when he's supposed to be at a party, I'm sure, but I'd better see if he needs anything. You stay here, dear. I shan't be long.'

Frances was wild with curiosity about the crash, but as her hosts seemed dead against her going outside she stayed where she was until Mrs Bates came back looking flushed and distinctly put out.

'What is it?' demanded Frances.

'Mr Harry skidded in the snow as he drove and crashed into the stable door, but he's quite all right. So is the car, but the stable doors will need rehanging, I shouldn't wonder.'

'Can I do anything?'

'No, dear. I'll have to leave you for a few minutes. Bates has gone to draw up the fire in the library over at the house, and I'm just slipping over myself to take some of this soup for Mr Harry.'

'Why has he come home?' asked Frances curiously.

'I couldn't say, dear.' Mrs Bates pulled on her coat and picked up her basket. 'From what I could see bed's the best place for him at the moment.'

She hurried off, and Frances pulled a face left on her own. She could hardly barge in over at the house unasked, even if she were consumed by curiosity, so she went into the kitchen to wash up the dinner things instead. She had just finished when Bates returned.

'Mr Harry's not very well. My wife's a bit worried, known him from a baby, of course. Tends to fuss over him.'

Frances hesitated. 'Would it be any good if I went over to see him, do you think?'

Bates shook his head doubtfully. 'I really couldn't say. Myself, I think he could do with cheering up, if you fancy having a shot at it.'

'Then I'll try. I can always beat a strategic retreat if he's not well enough to want company.' Frances ran upstairs to collect her sheepskin coat, and went down to find Mrs Bates had returned, looking upset.

'Bates says you're going over there, Miss Frances. Try to get him to drink the soup, would you? He might do it for you. He just told me to go to bed and leave him alone.'

'Then why don't you?' said Frances gently. 'Perhaps I could have a key and let myself back in, then you can both go to bed. If Mr Harry kicks me out I'll be straight back anyway, but if he'd appreciate some company I'll stay for a bit.'

The key was handed over with gratitude, to her surprise. Obviously both Bates and his wife worried over Harry Curthoys as if he were the son they'd never had, and were pleased with Frances's offer to help.

'Is he hurt?' asked Frances.

'No, nothing like that—more depressed,' said Mrs Bates vaguely.

Frances went across to the house gingerly on her high

heels, annoyed with herself for forgetting to change her
shoes, and entered quietly. Bates had left lights on here and
there, but even so it felt eerie to walk through the big
shadowy rooms alone so late, and Frances was glad to reach
the library. She paused outside the door, leaving her coat on
a chair, then knocked loudly and went in.

Harry Curthoys was sprawled in one of the wing chairs
near the fire, staring into it. His face was thrown into gaunt
relief by the leaping flames, and when he turned to look at
Frances the faint smile on his face was not the friendly,
casual one she was accustomed to, but a faint sardonic lift of
his lips.

'And what in blazes are *you* doing here, Robin
Redbreast? Or are you one of those im-imaginary figments
people talk about?' His voice was thick and slurred, and
informed Frances instantly of one salient point the Bateses
had omitted to mention. Harry Curthoys was not ill or
injured, he was drunk.

'No. I'm real.' Frances advanced slowly from the
shadows into the flickering light from the fire and sat down
on the chair opposite Harry. 'Why are you sitting in the
dark?'

'Suits my mood,' he said solemnly. 'I *feel* dark.' He peered
at her with half-closed eyes. 'Can't understand why you're
here. It's New Year's Eve—you should be out celebrating
with your lover.'

'He's in Scotland and I came back to work. I thought you
wouldn't be back for a day or two yet.'

He nodded sagely several times. 'So that's why you
came—thought I wouldn't be here.'

Frances didn't bother to contradict him in his present
mood. 'I thought you would be seeing in the New Year at a
friend's party.'

'Couldn't stick more than an hour or so. Came home.
Sh—stopped off at the King's Arms and had a drink or two
with Jim.'

Or even half a dozen drinks, thought Frances, undecided
whether to feel sorry for him, or just amused.

'Jim told me to walk home, but I didn't. My private road anyway. Couldn't harm anyone on that, could I?' he asked plaintively. 'Trouble was, too much blasted snow. Got in my way. Misjudged the stable doors. Had a little crash. Did Bates tell you?'

'He didn't need to. I heard it.' Frances got up to inspect the tray on the desk. It held two flasks, one of soup, the other presumably coffee provided by the efficient Mrs Bates.

'How about tasting some of this soup?' asked Frances. 'I had some earlier on. It's very good.'

Harry shook his head, eyeing her malevolently. 'They sent you over to make me drink the bloody stuff, I suppose.'

'No, they didn't. I suggested coming to see if you'd like some company. Perhaps I'd better go back.'

'No! No, don't go yet. Talk to me.'

'Very well.' Frances sat down composedly. Harry stood up for a moment, swayed a little and decided to sit down again. He was wearing a dinner jacket, but his white shirt was open at the neck, his black tie dangling and his hair was wildly untidy.

'I'm a little under the weather,' he informed her with dignity.

'You mean you're sloshed,' she said bluntly.

Harry glared at her, then shrugged indifferently. 'S'right. Sloshed. Sh—stoned, and other terms not fit for delicate ears.'

'Why?'

'What do you mean, why?'

'For all I know it may be an annual habit of yours to get smashed every New Year's Eve, but if not, then why tonight? And why did you come home?'

Harry's slightly unfocused eyes rested on the slender figure in the red dress for some time, then a cunning smile spread over his thin face. 'I'll tell *you* if you'll tell *me*.'

'Tell you what?'

'The real reason why you came running back here, when any red-blooded female ought to be out merrymaking on New Year's Eve.'

Frances regarded him calmly, then shrugged. He might as well know now as later. 'I got jilted,' she said flatly.

Harry's smile gave way to a look of maudlin sympathy. 'No! Not by the accountant? Oh, bad luck. I can sympathise. That's my reason too.'

She frowned. 'You mean you got jilted *again*?'

'No, no, no.' He shook a finger at her impatiently. 'I was doing the crossword, you see.'

'The crossword.'

'In the morning paper,' he said patiently.

'I know the one. I do it myself quite often, but it doesn't make me hit the bottle if I can't finish it,' said Frances reasonably.

'Ah, but what do they print just above the crossword?'

'The births column.'

'Bullseye!' Harry clapped in approval.

'So?'

'This morning what do you think caught my eye while I was juggling with an anagram?'

'No idea. Tell me.'

'It was right there, in black and white—to Annabel and Hartley Breckenridge a son. A *son*! Isn't that a joke?' Harry thrust a hand through his hair and looked round wildly. 'I need a drink——'

'No, you don't,' said Frances firmly. 'Go on about Annabel—she was the lady who jilted you, wasn't she?'

He nodded, an ugly set to his mouth. 'The very same.'

'And you're upset because she's married someone else and given him a son?'

'Upset! Hah! It's the bloody great irony of the year.' He let out a mirthless crack of laughter. 'She wouldn't marry me and have *my* son, would she? Yet she swore she was in love with me! Then she marries this doddering old moneybags Breckenridge and promptly presents him with an heir. It's enough to make you laugh, isn't it?'

Frances studied his bitter face gravely. 'Do you still love her so much, then?'

Harry shook his head impatiently. 'You're missing the

point, my little robin. But then, you don't know the punchline of the joke.'

He stared into the fire in morose silence for a lengthy interval, until Frances began to wonder if he'd forgotten she was there, but eventually he began to talk again, his voice less slurred than before, in a low, rapid monotone she had to lean forward to hear clearly.

'I was a bit of a lad in my youth,' he began. 'No worse than anyone else—no drugs or anything heavy, just fast cars, parties, girls, the odd argument with waiters, a few chairs smashed up—you know the kind of thing.'

'Not first hand,' she said drily.

'Quite. Well, my father got pretty fed up with me. Threatened to cut off my allowance and all that, but I had some money of my own at the time, left by my grandmother, so his threats didn't carry much clout. Then, just before I finished at Cambridge my father fell off his horse. Just fell off, would you believe. Must have had a giddy spell, or something, but the horse kicked him in the temple and that was that.' Harry ran a hand over his face and was silent for a moment, then went on more slowly. 'I loved my father, and I knew quite well he loved me, for all his views on discipline and all that. What I never realised until his will was read was the extent of his passion for this place. The house and estate were entailed on me, anyway, but the money was his to dispose of as he wished. From his will it was crystal clear that he was afraid, if I inherited young, I'd spend everything on fast living in general and let the Court go to rack and ruin. So apart from an annuity to my mother and a small legacy to Charlotte, who was already married, he left the bulk of the money in trust.'

'Until you marry?'

He sighed. 'No. Until my first son is born. Not child—*son*. He obviously felt this would settle me down, make sure I joined the ranks of the serious-minded. My first reaction was a blinding hurt that he hadn't trusted me sufficiently to assume my responsibilities when the time came. Then I got angry and decided to earn the money myself. With the remains of the legacy from my grandmother, and a sum my mother insisted on putting up, I set up as an estate agent in Astcote where I knew the Curthoys name still carried some weight, and after several years, and a lot of hard graft, I began to do nicely, able to keep the old house in reasonable nick, with a skeleton staff in the winter and a few more in the summer once I decided to open the place to the public to earn some of its keep. Then I met Annabel.'

'So what went wrong?' asked Frances.

'The terms of the will had never been made public, but I knew it was generally held that I had to marry to get the money. Annabel told me she knew all about the strings attached to my inheritance, and would be happy to marry me. Like a fool I deluded myself into believing she knew the truth, was willing to marry me and live in comparatively reduced circumstances until the necessary son arrived.' Harry smiled bitterly. 'It was only when Mother arrived for the wedding and congratulated Annabel on being such a good sport about having babies until she achieved a son that all was revealed. We were having dinner. I shall never eat duck in orange sauce again without seeing the utterly appalled expression on Annabel's face.'

'She thought she just had to walk down the aisle to hit the jackpot,' said Frances prosaically.

'Absolutely.' Harry grinned evilly. 'Before you could say Jack Robinson—why *does* one say Jack Robinson?— Annabel had given me back the ring, with reluctance, and departed, hot foot to get a notice in the paper that the wedding was off. Next thing I knew she'd married Hartley Breckenridge—old American banking money. She even wrote to me. Told me he was rich enough to give her anything she wanted, and old enough to make children out of the question. Her mistake, unless she's planted a cuckoo in the Breckenridge nest. The fact remains that if she'd married *me* that son could have been mine and I'd have the money to repair the roof.'

Frances regarded him thoughtfully, undecided whether Harry was grieving for his lost love or the money. 'Why haven't you asked someone else to marry you?'

His look was derisive. 'For what it was worth, I was in love with Annabel. Since then I've never met anyone else I fancied sharing my life with—and even if I had, who would be fool enough to agree once I told my touching little story?'

Frances shook her head sadly. 'Where I come from it's simpler. One falls in love with a man and just marries him—if he asks—regardless of his expectations.'

'Sounds like Utopia.'

'No. It's a small village near Warwick.'

Harry chuckled and got up to inspect the tray. 'I think I could eat some of this soup now. My outpourings have made me hungry. My apologies to you, Frances. Must have bored you to tears.'

'No indeed. I found it almost as fascinating as Hal's story.'

'Thanks for the "almost"! Have some soup?'

'Not for me, thank you. I ate an enormous meal with the Bateses.' Frances looked on with approval as Harry filled a mug with steaming soup and took it back to the fire to drink. 'Feel a little better now?'

He smiled ruefully. 'If you mean am I sober now, I rather think I am. Which reminds me—God, I'm a self-centred lout! You said you'd been jilted. Tell me what happened.'

She looked away. 'Nothing to make a fuss about——'

'Like me, you mean!'

Frances gave him a crooked little smile. 'Let's say I didn't get drunk and I brought the Morris home in one piece, anyway.'

Harry sighed. 'Only myself to blame. Now, why has this fool of an accountant broken it off?'

'The usual reason. He found someone else—a lady accountant he met at the office. They're having an engagement party right this minute.'

'Hell's bells!' Harry stared at her appalled, then got up quickly. 'Come on, Frances, let's have a drink. Several, in fact. It's New Year's Eve, and since we both have sorrows to drown, I vote we drown them together.'

'Have some coffee first,' she advised.

'Anything you say.' Harry filled two cups from the flask, then added generous measures of brandy, and in silence they sat sipping the hot liquid, both of them content to stare into the flames in companionable silence until the church bells began pealing in the distance.

Harry pulled Frances to her feet and poured more brandy into two snifters. 'Let's drink a toast, Frances. May the New Year bring happiness to us both.'

'Happiness to us both,' she echoed and tossed off the neat brandy in one gulp, as Harry did, then gasped for breath.

He laughed indulgently as she spluttered, then took her glass and put it down, his head on one side as he regarded her questioningly. 'Am I to be granted the privilege of a kiss to welcome in the New Year?'

Frances blinked, then smiled diffidently, and held up her face to be kissed. Harry Curthoys was only a little over six feet tall, but he had to lean down quite a way to kiss the mouth offered up to him so trustingly. Putting his hands lightly either side of her waist he bent to touch her mouth gently with his own, which lingered involuntarily before he drew back a little, his eyes meeting hers. Frances breathed in sharply, her lips parting as she saw the startled look on his face, then she shut her eyes blindly as he bent his head and kissed her again, much less fleetingly.

There was nothing hurried or perfunctory about the way his lips coaxed hers apart then deepened their pressure, and Frances stood utterly still as he drew her closer and slid a hand down her back to fit her body into his as he leaned over her, his mouth moving in a way that made it impossible not to respond as his tongue slid along hers, and her breathing quickened in answer to the rhythm of his. The arms holding her tightened, the mouth on hers grew more demanding, and wildly Frances tried to remember that this was Harry Curthoys, not Chris, that he had drunk far more than was good for him, and was making use of her as substitute for his precious Annabel, and several other reasons why they shouldn't be doing what they were doing. Only it was so wonderfully comforting, positive balm to her wounds, to be held like this and have her hurt kissed better. When Harry finally held her a little away from him Frances blinked up at him, dazed.

'Should I say I'm sorry, Frances?' he asked, in an unsteady, husky voice.

'I don't know.' She looked down, staring hard at the toes of her black shoes. 'Are you? Sorry, I mean?'

'For kissing you, definitely not. But if I annoyed you, upset you in any way, then yes, I am.'

'You didn't.'

'I'm glad.' He put a gentle fingertip under her chin and lifted her face to look into her eyes. 'Happy New Year, Frances.'

She looked for a long moment into the narrow grey eyes below the dishevelled fair hair, then relaxed. 'Happy New Year, Harry.'

He smiled, in a way that recalled pictures of that other, devil-may-care Harry of old, and waved her to her chair. 'Then as you're not about to black my eye will you stay and talk a while?'

'Yes. Only let's not talk about, well, sad things. Tell me what happens at Curthoys Court when it's open during the summer, what kind of Christmas you had with your sister, what type of properties you sell——'

'Done,' he said promptly, and poured more brandy in their glasses, laughing at her wary expression. 'We'll sip these very slowly, then we won't be lured into further temptation.'

'Temptation?'

He scratched his nose, eyeing her candidly. 'Well, if I were really honest—do you want me to be honest?'

Frances gave it some thought as she took a sip of her brandy.

'Yes, I think so.'

'In that case I feel I should explain that the kiss just now was meant to be a cheery little peck, short and sweet to

mark the occasion. There's not much point in trying to
deny it didn't turn out quite like that.'

'Very true.'

'In fact, I could have gone on kissing you indefinitely if
I'd thought there was any chance of your letting me.' His
eyes gleamed very bright over the rim of his glass.

'I didn't offer much resistance,' she pointed out.

'You were taken by surprise. But then,' he added, 'so was
I. Kissing you *is* very surprising.'

'Why?'

'Your response was quite a shock to my system—sent my
blood pressure rocketing sky high.'

Frances shot a worried look at him. 'I didn't have
anything to do with the response. It just happened.'

'Does it happen every time?'

'You've only kissed me once.'

'With anyone else I'd take that as an invitation—all
right, pax.' He held up a hand at her indignant scowl. 'I
know you didn't mean it that way. I'm just curious to know
if that same reaction occurs every time you're kissed.'

Frances had been kissed as much as most girls, sometimes
with her co-operation, sometimes not, and by Chris a great
deal, as was only natural, but none of the kisses had ever
startled her in quite the same way. A kiss was just a kiss, as
the song said. Except when Harry Curthoys practised the
art, apparently.

'No, not every time,' she said evasively.

There was an odd look in Harry's eyes. 'Only on New
Year's Eve, perhaps?'

Frances smiled. 'There is something special about
ushering in the New Year, isn't there?' Then she sobered.
'This one has been more unusual than most, I think, one
way and another.'

'Are you very unhappy, Frances?' The tenderness in
Harry's voice was almost her undoing, and she had to
swallow hard.

'I'd be lying if I said no.' She lifted her chin and smiled
valiantly. 'But I know perfectly well that the hurt will

lessen as time goes on. It's just that it's a bit difficult when the man in question happens to live next door to one's family. Embarrassing all round.'

'Then don't go home for a while. Stay here over the weekends as much as you wish,' he suggested.

'Thank you. I will.' She smiled gratefully, then remembered a happier piece of news. 'By the way, my father and Jassy are over the moon—there's a new little Wilding in the offing next June.' She bit her lip as a shadow passed over Harry's face. 'I'm sorry. You can't want to hear about more happy arrivals.'

'I'm very pleased for you.'

There was silence for a while after that. Harry seemed to retreat into the depression of earlier on, and Frances cursed her own lack of tact. 'Have I made you miserable again by talking about babies?' she ventured, and to her relief he laughed.

'No, of course not. Actually I was thinking about the roof, and which bank I should rob to pay for the re-leading that's needed.'

'Is it that bad?'

'Yes, Frances Wilding. It's that bad. I must find some way to raise the money, and soon, at that.' He smiled ruefully. 'I apologise. You wanted to talk about pleasant things and here I am, depressing the hell out of you.'

'If it helps I don't mind,' she assured him. 'When I said "pleasant things" I think I meant anything other than our respective love lives.'

'How right you are.' Harry reached over and topped up her glass. 'Let's forget about old flames and concentrate on Frances Wilding and Harry Curthoys. May their shadows never grow less. Your health, Frances.' He raised his glass and drank deeply.

Frances eyed the contents of her glass with misgiving, then told herself that once a year a little over-indulgence was permissible. She toasted the man watching her. 'Your health, Harry.'

'I suppose you wouldn't care to come and sit on my knee?' he asked.

Frances sat up very straight. 'That's the drink talking!'

'No, it's not, it's me. Harry. Well—would you?'

Frances gave his request all the due solemn consideration of three glasses of brandy, which was two more than she had ever drunk in her life. 'I think I would like to sit on your knee, but that's probably because I've had far too much to drink.'

'Very likely,' he agreed gloomily. 'I must say it's a bit deflating to learn you have to be stoned out of your mind before you find me attractive enough to sit on my lap.'

'No, no, you misunderstood me.' Her eyes widened at him ingenuously. 'I know very well that I do want to sit on your knee, *and* be cuddled a little, but sober I wouldn't have dreamed of admitting it.'

'I would dearly love to—cuddle you a little,' he said softly, and made no move from his half-supine position in his chair. 'But you'd have to come over here of your own accord.'

'You expect rather a lot, Mr Curthoys.'

'Not expect. Hope.'

Harry gazed into her eyes steadily in the shadowy, firelit room, and Frances stared back, mesmerised, conscious of a definite pull towards him. He lay back in his chair on the other side of the hearth, his posture utterly relaxed, yet she felt the will he was imposing on her as strongly as though he had her by the hands, drawing her towards him. She rose slowly to her feet and moved across the space separating them.

'I should go home,' she said huskily.

Harry shook his head and held out his arms. 'That isn't why you got up, Frances.'

She hesitated, a helpless, pleading look on her face. 'Please——'

He reached up and caught her wrists, and she fell into his embrace, curling against him as he drew her across his thighs and held her close, smoothing her hair as her head came to rest against his shoulder.

'I won't hurt you, Frances. But I think we both need a little human contact tonight. I know I do. Just to have you here like this is a comfort. Do you feel the same?'

Frances was not at all sure how she felt. It was pleasant, and more than pleasant, to be held close in Harry's arms like this. She was conscious of warmth from the fire, warmth from the brandy, warmth from the security of the arms encircling her. She sighed a little and lifted her head to tell him, but his mouth came down on hers and the impulse to speak left her. The world contracted, grew smaller, encapsulated into this warm, secure haven of Harry's arms, of his mouth moving on hers, his arms right around her. Then his hand moved and her breath drew in sharply as his slim fingers slowly traced the shape of her breast, their touch burning through the fine wool until his fingertips closed on the nipple that rose to their touch even through its covering, and Frances gasped. Harry made a stifled sound deep in his throat as his tongue caressed hers and his breathing grew ragged. When he tore his mouth away her eyes stared up into his, wide with wonder, and the little golden streaks in the brown irises shone like tiny flames in the half-light.

'Frances——' he began breathlessly, and at the sound of his voice her lids dropped and she turned her head away, her body stiffening in his grasp. 'Don't turn away from me,' he urged. 'Not tonight.'

'What are you asking?' she whispered.

'Only that you stay a little longer, just like this. Nothing more, I promise. Not even a kiss. Just simple human contact, on a night when we both need it.'

'So you can pretend I'm Annabel?'

Harry shook his head emphatically. 'No. Never that. Not my idea of good manners. I'm fully aware that I have Miss Frances Wilding here in my arms, and I'm very conscious of my good fortune. Will you stay for a bit—please?'

Frances wasn't proof against the entreaty in Harry's

voice, and she sighed a little and nodded. 'Yes. For a little while.'

Harry Curthoys settled himself more comfortably in the big chair, gently shifting the girl in his arms until she lay relaxed against him, her head on his shoulder, his chin on her ruffled curls. A log fell, and sparks streamed up the chimney, but neither of them stirred. As others in the outside world celebrated the arrival of the New Year with inebriated revelry, the inmates of Curthoys Court grew utterly still and silent as they fell asleep in each other's arms.

CHAPTER SIX

FRANCES woke because her legs were cold and her neck was stiff. It was dark, and for a moment she had no idea where she was. Then she tried to move and found she was entwined with a sleeping Harry to such an extent that it took some time to extricate herself. When she finally broke free she hugged her arms across her chest, shivering in the faint grey light that had begun to steal through the window. Then she went silently from the room to get her coat, afraid to switch on a light in case she woke Harry. The last thing she wanted was to meet him face to face in the cool, cruel light of dawn. She thrust one arm into the sleeve of her coat then hesitated and took it out again. Stealthily she crept back into the library and laid the coat over the sleeping figure, then hurried from the room and through the house, turning off the lights that had been burning all night.

She opened the great outer door and gasped as the wind hurled a gust of snowflakes in her face, then closed the door carefully behind her before dashing across the court, head bowed against the wind tearing through the thin wool of her dress. By the time she reached the gatehouse her teeth were chattering and her fingers so numb she had difficulty getting the key into the lock. When she finally managed to get the door open the light went on, to her dismay, and she looked up into the disapproving eyes of Mrs Bates, who was stationed half-way up the stairs.

'Miss Frances! Have you been out all night?'

It was the last straw. Frances felt weary, depressed, her head was splitting and, unless she was much mistaken, quite sure Mrs Bates thought she'd spent the night in Harry's bed. She burst into tears, rubbing her knuckles in her eyes miserably.

Mrs Bates descended the stairs hurriedly, and swept the girl into her ample embrace. 'There, there, don't take on so, my dear. What is it? Whatever's the matter? Surely Mr Harry didn't——?'

'No!' Frances drew away to explain, her voice choked. It all came out in a rush, punctuated by sobs: her own unhappiness over Chris, Harry's about Annabel's new son. 'We just talked, and drank some brandy, and the fire was warm and we just—just fell asleep,' she finished, and sniffed loudly. 'He's still there in the library.'

'But where's your coat—you're like ice, child.'

'I put it over Mr Harry—it was so cold this morning.'

Instantly mollified, Mrs Bates shooed her upstairs.

'Turn on your blanket then undress as fast as you can and get into bed while I make you a nice hot cup of tea.'

Frances thanked her fervently and dived upstairs, brushing her teeth and washing her face while the electric blanket began to do its work. Minutes later, in her striped Laura Ashley pyjamas, she huddled under the duvet, feeling the warmth stealing through her body with rapture and keeping her mind a determined blank about the events of the night. With gratitude she accepted the tea tray Mrs Bates brought her, and ate the biscuits and took the aspirins tactfully provided before drinking two cups of tea. Then at last she settled down to relax in the warm bed. After a while she switched off the blanket and lay watching the snow feathering past the leaded panes of the windows as the cold wintry light gradually replaced the darkness.

Frances made her first New Year's resolution as she lay there. She would avoid brandy in future if the result of drinking it was the irresponsibility she had shown last night. She must have been mad to let Harry Curthoys kiss her. And she was uneasily aware that 'let' was not all that accurate a verb, either. 'Encouraged' was probably nearer the mark. Harry had had an excuse. He'd been fairly tight to start with. But she had not. She should have had the sense to come away when he sobered up—that first kiss that was supposed to wish her Happy New Year should have been warning enough. But no, thought Frances bitterly, she had to stay and perform her cork-shoulder act for Harry Curthoys, of course, and look where it had landed her. Not in his bed, admittedly, which was something, but a night spent on a man's lap was hardly the type of behaviour calculated to foster a pleasant, impersonal employer-employee relationship. Frances groaned and turned her face to the wall, and abruptly Chris's face was in her mind and she began to cry hopelessly, feeling suddenly lost, with no niche in her life for her to fit into neatly, as once she had had. Now Chris had Isla, Dad had Jassy, even Harry had Curthoys Court and a definite place in life. Whereas Frances Wilding felt like a displaced person.

It was past eleven when Frances woke from a brief, heavy sleep that left her unrefreshed and wondering how to cope with the new turn of events. Would Harry be different? Awkward with her, perhaps? Or maybe he wouldn't remember anything about the night before when he woke. Frances was not left long in doubt. When she arrived downstairs no one was in the gatehouse, but her sheepskin coat was hanging over the back of a chair in the parlour with a note thrust through the buttonhole. It said, 'Come and see me when you feel like it. I'm nursing a hangover in the morning-room. H.'

One look at the weather when she got up had decided Frances on comfort in preference to elegance, and she was wearing a fleece-lined tracksuit over a thick sweater, with socks inside her boots to keep her feet warm as she dashed over to the Court, huddled in her coat. She stamped her feet outside before going into the entrance hall, almost colliding with Bates as she went on into the great hall.

'Ah, good morning, Miss Frances—you found your coat then.' The man smiled at her kindly. 'I was surprised to find it draped over Mr Harry in the library this morning. Dead to the world he was.'

'I still am,' said a sepulchral voice, and Harry appeared, looking very wan and haggard as he clutched at his head.

'Never again,' he said bitterly. 'Bates, if I ask for brandy in future ignore me!'

Bates chuckled. 'Why not take Miss Frances back into the morning-room and sit by the fire? I believe my wife has coffee ready.'

'Best news I've had this morning—thank you.' Harry took Frances by the elbow. 'How are you today? Not very talkative, that's plain.'

'I'm all right.'

'Just all right?'

She nodded, then smiled faintly and he smiled back, relieved, as he opened the morning-room door for her. He sniffed ecstatically at the scent of fresh coffee, and the awkwardness Frances had felt at encountering him again evaporated as she busied herself with the cups, putting in a dash of milk and one lump of sugar before giving Harry his.

'You know my tastes already,' he said, and sat back in his chair, eyeing her uneasily. 'Frances, did I, er, get out of hand last night?'

She felt her cheeks grow warm. 'Don't you remember?'

He gave her a hunted look. 'I remember kissing you and holding you in my arms in the chair in front of the fire. Next thing I knew, Bates was fighting me for your coat, which I refused to give up without a struggle, apparently. Probably thought it was you. He was a bit po-faced about finding me asleep in the library in broad daylight still in the DJ and black tie, and using your coat for a blanket. When did you—I mean, how long did you stay with me? Or was the entire episode the product of my drunken imagination?'

Frances relaxed. 'No, you didn't imagine it. I didn't wake up myself until it was getting light. It was icy cold in the library by that time, so I left you my coat and ran back to the gatehouse.'

'In just that red dress?'

She nodded, pulling a face. 'It was freezing and I had a terrible job to get the key in the lock, then when I managed to open the door there was Mrs Bates on the stairs in the most awesome dressing-gown with her hair in a plait and a face like thunder.'

Harry groaned loudly and covered his eyes with his hands.

'So now she thinks you spent the night sleeping with me!'

'I did,' Frances pointed out.

He stole a look at her. 'How did you explain?'

She described her tears and her confession and how Mrs Bates had become instantly motherly and comforting.

'Perhaps *I* should have tried tears—she wasn't very comforting to me,' he said morosely.

'Ah, but I didn't get drunk in the village and crash into the stable doors!'

'Don't rub it in—I feel low enough as it is!'

'Sorry—didn't mean to be nasty.'

'Frances, I can't visualise your being nasty under any circumstances.'

She grinned at him. 'That's because you don't know me very well.'

Harry's face was thoughtful. 'After last night I feel I know you a little better than I did.'

Frances stared at him indignantly. 'What do you mean?'

'Steady on—don't get your feathers ruffled. I meant that all that stuff I poured out into your captive ears last night is something I normally keep to myself. Must have bored you to death.'

'On the contrary. I only wish there was something I could do to help.'

Harry sighed. 'You could always drive the getaway car for me when I rob the bank.'

Frances giggled. 'And a lot better than you, if last night is anything to go by!'

'I shall ignore your cruel jibes,' he said with dignity, then grinned. 'Want to come out and inspect the damage with me?'

'It's time I started work—I'm late enough as it is.'

'Not today, Josephine—it's New Year's Day, a holiday, so come and help me mend the stable doors instead.'

Bundled up in her sheepskin coat, with her woollen cap crammed down over her curls Frances crunched through the snow with Harry to inspect the damage, which was less than expected considering the noise the crash had made. She held nails and screws, and stamped her feet on the snow-covered ground while Harry repaired the hinges, which had suffered most in the impact. Some of the wood was splintered as well, but Mason was the chap for that, Harry told her cheerfully, and challenged her to a snowball fight. Frances agreed with delight, and gave as good as she got in the pelting match that followed until one particularly accurate missile from Harry caught her off balance and she landed on her back in a snowdrift, gasping for breath and laughing helplessly. He hauled her to her feet swiftly, dusting her down and demanding whether she was hurt, but Frances assured him it took more than a mere lucky fluke to put her out of action, then had to sprint off in hasty retreat as he threatened to renew his attack.

They were still breathless when they got back to the house, but Harry's headache was gone and Frances felt a hundred per cent better than earlier, and they both did full justice to the spaghetti carbonara Mrs Bates had made for lunch.

'I think we're both remarkable,' said Harry, when they were at the coffee stage.

'Oh? In what way?'

'Well, there's you with your very recently battered heart, and me with my wounded pride, and look how stiff our upper lips are about the whole thing.'

Frances made a face. 'I wasn't terribly cheerful when I finally got to bed this morning, I'm afraid. But I know very well there's no point in wallowing in self-pity, so I'll just have to get on with life and think of Chris as just an old friend instead of—of——'

'Lover?'

'Not the word I was looking for. I was about to say husband, I suppose. Not that we had planned to marry for ages. Yet with Isla, the new lady-love, Chris is in a tremendous hurry, which is a bit hard on my ego.'

Harry leaned towards her and took one of her hands. 'Are you very much in love with the chap, Frances?'

She looked steadily into the intent grey eyes, then frowned. '"In love" doesn't seem quite the right way to describe us, either. It's just that it's always been Chris all my life, ready to fight my battles in school, give me a hand with my homework, teach me to swim—oh, I don't know, it's hard to explain. I suppose that I'm trying to say that Chris has always been *there*. And now he isn't, and won't be ever again, and it's very like losing part of myself.'

Harry's clasp tightened. 'The feeling will pass, I promise, Frances. I know it's hard to imagine at the moment.'

'No, I know you're right.' Frances withdrew her hand gently. 'And you're very kind to listen to my misery and woe.'

'Not a bit of it—I subjected you to enough of mine last night.' Harry's eyes held hers. 'But when the going gets rough, when you feel more down than usual, don't keep it to yourself. Tell me. I know what it's like, so don't be afraid to admit you need cheering up.'

She smiled gratefully. 'Thank you.'

'Right—now what would you like to do this afternoon? It's stopped snowing, so we could go for a walk, or we could watch some television, or play records——'

'You don't have to entertain me, you know. I came back here to work.'

Harry shook his head decisively. 'Work is out for today. And I'd be very grateful for your company, so what shall it be?'

Frances glanced towards the window. 'I think there's a glimmer of sun out there. I'd like a walk, only no more snowballs, please.'

'Done.'

They left the warmth of the house for the diamond-bright light outside and crunched through the snow of the stableyard towards the drive, which provided a fairly secure surface for walking. Frances could feel the warmth rising in her cheeks as they kept up an energetic pace, and Harry cast an eye at the sky and sniffed the air.

'I fancy there's a bit more to come yet—good thing I came back yesterday after all. Might not have made it home if I'd left it much longer.'

'You could have stayed with your friends.'

'I know. But I get restless if I'm away from here for long. I hated being sent away to school and couldn't wait to get back in the holidays. I used to bring friends with me sometimes, but I never went to stay at their homes, however much I was asked. I begrudged every second spent away. Annabel and I used to argue about it. She wanted a house in town as well. More of the bright lights and less of the country air.'

Privately Frances considered Harry was well shot of the fair Annabel, but kept her views to herself as they walked, skirting the house in a great sweep, but always able to see it as Harry led her along various side paths that brought them in a rough circle from their starting point. Frances realised that their route would take them past the church, and her pulse quickened as unconsciously she accelerated her pace, slithering a little at times on the slippery surface of the track.

'Hey!' Harry grabbed her arm as she almost slipped. 'You're in a great hurry all of a sudden. Cold?'

'No, not in the least,' she said breathlessly, and widened her eyes at him in appeal. 'Could we go into the church? Please?'

Harry stopped, and eyed her quizzically. 'Is that why you wanted to come out? To visit Hal?'

'No,' she said stoutly, but he grinned, shaking his head.

'Liar! I don't have the keys on me——'

'Could we go back and get them?'

'Oh, very well,' he agreed reluctantly. 'But it'll be as cold as——'

'The grave?' she said, giggling.

'Absolutely!'

They hurried back to the house, where the kitchen smelt

tantalisingly of freshly baked scones and roasting meat. Mrs Bates looked up expectantly from the pastry she was rolling out.

'Ready for your tea, Mr Harry?'

'*I* am,' he said pointedly, 'but this young lady yearns to visit the church, so not being one to mock at the religious tendencies of others I suppose I'd better take her there.'

'In this weather?' Mrs Bates shook her head in disapproval. 'Well, don't stay too long, Miss Frances, or you'll catch a chill.'

Harry took Frances's hand in his and ran with her along the path to the church, which was hidden from the house by a copse of yew trees. He unlocked the door and turned the heavy wrought-iron handle. With a screeching of hinges the door swung open, and he switched on some of the lights. The dim interior sprang to life and Frances stepped carefully over the memorial stone of a long-dead Curthoys in the doorway, pausing for a moment at the Norman font, where the position of the hinge and fastener for the original cover was still faintly visible. The atmosphere was heavy with the smell of old wood and leather, overlaid with a faint hint of incense even now, and Frances shivered a little in the cold, which seemed more intense now they were inside the church.

'Don't hang about too long, Frances, it's like a damn deep-freeze in here,' complained Harry, and jogged up and down on the spot to keep warm. 'Go on, take a look at Hal—which is why you came—and for God's sake let's go back before my blood congeals in my veins.'

From where they were standing at the back of the church Frances could see rows of pews, the stained-glass window over the altar, the surprisingly simple wrought-iron cross and candlesticks, some hatchment boards on the walls with Curthoys armorial bearings on them, and to the left of the pulpit the first of the tombs. But she knew only too well that it was necessary to walk up the aisle and turn into the small side chapel before she could renew her acquaintance with Hal Curthoys, and now she was here it was rather difficult to make the effort alone, since Harry plainly had no intention of accompanying her. As she went down the aisle she gave a tentative look over her shoulder at him, but he just smiled mockingly and waved her on. Frances lifted her chin and marched smartly past the front pew, and then came to a sudden halt. The side chapel was in darkness.

'Sorry,' called Harry, and pressed another switch, illuminating the chapel and the railed, recumbent figure with a sudden drama that took Frances's breath away. The sheer beauty of the effigy drew her like a magnet, and without realising she had moved she was clutching the railing separating the tomb from the others, gazing at the earthly reminder of the long-dead Hal Curthoys. The skill of the sculptor had wrought a memorial of such indolent, relaxed grace there was no suggestion of death in the posture of the body. Even in its deep repose it gave an impression of vitality and slim, muscular strength, and she forgot the cold, seized with an overwhelming urge to touch, to stroke, to smooth the lovelocks away from the hidden face.

'Boo!' said Harry in her ear, and Frances almost jumped out of her skin.

'Idiot!' she stormed, turning on him, then stopped dead, her colour high as she remembered that this was her employer, the man who paid her wages. 'I'm sorry,' she said stiffly. 'You startled me.'

Harry's eyebrows rose as he took her by the arm to leave.

'There's no rule against you bawling me out if you feel like it, Frances!'

She bit her lip. 'I forgot you were, well——'

'Your boss?'

'Well, yes, but the fact that you're the owner of all this, and—' she gestured over her shoulder towards Hal's tomb, '—his descendant as well. I didn't mean to be rude.'

Harry gave her an irritable little push in the direction of the door. 'Don't talk such rot, Frances. You'll be touching your forelock and curtsying next.' He turned off the lights and locked the door, then ran with her back to the house, both of them slithering in places and gasping in the bite of the rising wind.

'I don't know that I'd go as far as that,' she shouted, and took a firm hold on her red knitted cap, which was threatening to take off.

'You'd better not!' he yelled back, and threw open the kitchen door.

From then on life took on a routine that helped Frances no end in her efforts to reshape her life without Chris. She buckled down to her work on the records with a will, and spent her days utterly absorbed in the past. There were no more dramatic revelations about Arabella and her crime, it was true, but even without the passion and anguish of the hidden diary Frances had more than enough to keep her interest centred firmly on the seventeenth century, which went a long way towards making her life happier in the twentieth.

Frances dined with Harry Curthoys two, sometimes three evenings a week, and on Sundays, unless he were away, he fell into the habit of taking her for a stroll down to the King's Arms for a pre-lunch drink, a practice duly noted and accepted by the regulars of the pub. Some days Frances's campaign of rehabilitation suffered a set-back, notably on the receipt of letters from Chris apologising and justifying his change of heart. On the first occasion Harry was home to dinner and quick to notice and remedy her low spirits, but when the second letter came Harry was away and Frances worked off the effects of Chris's epistle by sheer physical effort up in the attic, sorting and tidying and delving into trunks and boxes until she was so tired and dirty all she wanted was a bath, her dinner and sleep.

It irritated Frances to read that Chris apparently found her blessing necessary for his relationship with the clever and beautiful Isla, begging her to write to him to reassure him of her good wishes for his future. Some people wanted jam on it, thought Frances angrily and dashed off a quick note to the effect that as far as she was concerned Chris could walk into the sunset with his bonny Highland lassie with no misgivings about the welfare of good old Frances, the girl next door.

'Are you all right?' demanded her father during the weekly call from home.

'I'm fine. Working hard and enjoying it very much.'

'And your Mr Curthoys—still treating you well?'

'Very well indeed. I'm lucky to have such a fascinating job. How's Jassy?'

'Blooming. But she worries about you.'

'Tell her it isn't necessary. Really, Dad.'

'Do we see you some time in the future?'

Frances paused. 'Not yet—not while the weather's so dicey. We've had a lot of snow here.'

'But don't the weekends drag, sweetheart?'

'No chance. Don't worry about me, Dad, I'm not going into a decline or anything, I promise you.'

Which was the truth. And the weekends did not drag. If Harry were home Frances spent some of the time with him. If not she worked most of the time, which brought much disapproval from the Bateses down on her head, but gave her mind the distraction it needed to avoid repining about Chris.

As winter finally relented and made way for spring Frances saw rather less of Harry, who seemed to be working himself into the ground one way and another. As the property market began to move up a gear he was home less to dinner, and the Sunday visits to the King's Arms stopped too, to her regret, when Harry began opening his office on Sunday mornings in addition to the rest of the week. He became thinner and less high-spirited, though unfailingly friendly and courteous to Frances on the now infrequent occasions spent in her company. Even in his spare time Harry was involved in getting the Court ready for its Easter opening to the public and Frances missed the evenings spent in conversation with him over the dinner table, even though meals on a tray in her bedroom at the gatehouse were a thing of the past since New Year's Eve.

'I'm worried about Mr Harry,' said Mrs Bates one

evening. 'He's overdoing things.'

'Always the same just before the house opens,' agreed her husband. 'Sometimes I think his father must have been a bit soft in the head to leave him this place with no money to run it.'

'I don't know why he doesn't just get married,' said Mrs Bates. 'It would solve a lot of problems, but that Miss Hayward put him off the whole idea good and proper.'

Frances made no comment, inwardly surprised that neither of them knew the precise terms of the will. Obviously only close family were in the know, plus the fickle Annabel, who presumably kept quiet about them to avoid appearing in a bad light to her friends.

'Mrs Bates thinks you're overdoing things,' Frances informed Harry over their roast lamb the following Sunday evening.

He sighed. 'What choice do I have! Anyway, you're a fine one to talk. I have it from the same reliable source that you even worked after dinner last night, when all sensible people were either out socialising or sprawled in front of the television.'

Frances was unrepentant. 'The Court will be open in three weeks and I'm determined to have a complete display ready on the Civil War period by then, otherwise there's not much point in your working overtime to get the coffin room ready to display it in.'

'Muniment room, if you don't mind, Miss Wilding.'

'Oops, sorry.'

'Anyway, don't try to change the subject. Saturday evenings are taboo for poring over all those records, Frances.' His thin face was very serious as he poured wine into her glass.

'I wasn't. I was in the library, going through the catalogue I've made.' Frances's eyes sparkled with enthusiasm. 'Since the only archives ready are the Stuart ones I thought we could display a few well-chosen volumes of the same period on the library table. You know, carelessly strewn about as though someone was in the middle of reading them.'

Harry nodded appreciatively. 'Good idea.'

'And yesterday in the attic I found a bible box that just needs a new hinge and a new piece of glass in the display lid. The Stuart bible will go in there nicely. Then you have a very old edition of Foxe's *Book of Martyrs* that can lie open on the lectern with the eagle—why are you smiling at me like that?' she demanded.

'Your enthusiasm—it's wonderful!'

'But don't you agree it's a good idea?'

'I do, I do.' He held up his hands in mock-defence. 'Believe me, if it'll attract more people with entrance money in their hot little hands I'll be delighted.'

'It's bound to, especially school trips and so on. Any history students will be interested in the reading habits of the Curthoys family of the period, which were probably fairly representative of the tastes of the time.' Frances took a deep breath. 'I haven't mentioned this before, but I'm now fairly sure I've tracked down the book Hal was reading when he—he——'

'Snuffed it,' supplied Harry inelegantly, but his eyes gleamed. 'How did you track down that little bit of information?'

'Well, I can't prove it, of course, but the new books bought at this time were recorded by my darling Pegler in the household accounts. You have a number of very valuable editions here, as I said, like the translations of St Ambrose and Virgil, which pre-date Hal, but there were only two books actually bought in the time between his arrival home and the time of his death; a new issue of *The Wise Men of Gotham* and a new translation of *The Golden Ass of Apuleius*, both of which are in almost mint condition, except that the latter has two pages very badly stained and discoloured near the middle, which could be the result of having lain open on the grass,' she finished in triumph.

Harry whistled.

'Then by all means let us display it, my clever little

sleuth, with a label saying something like, "Believed to be the book, Hal Curthoys was reading . . ." and so on. God knows, I'd like to publish Arabella's diary, but since that's out, one way and another, a bit of colour added to Hal's mysterious demise won't go amiss.'

'Couldn't the Astcote *Weekly Gazette* do a piece on it?' suggested Frances. 'You must be a very good customer with all the property advertising space you buy. They could write about the new attractions about to be revealed at Curthoys Court, and include details of the book, complete with grass stain.'

'Good idea! I'll get Tony Latimer to come along and take some photographs, he's quite good at it, and writes very well. God knows I need something to draw the crowds—I don't think the roof will survive another winter. Bates told me today there are leaks in one of the attics where the lead has cracked. All that snow this year was the last straw.'

'What will you do?'

'A temporary patch-up job for now, but it's only postponing the evil day, I'm afraid.'

'Can't you borrow money?'

Harry smiled bleakly. 'How would I pay it back?'

Frances looked crestfallen, and she sighed. 'I just wish there was some way to help.'

'You're doing very well, Frances, more than I could possibly have expected, particularly in return for the joke of a salary I pay you.'

'You provide bed and board, remember, and I never have time to spend much otherwise.'

'Then you should,' Harry said promptly. 'Is that why your hair is longer? Because you don't have time to get it cut?'

She coloured. 'I always have it done in the same place at home, and I meant to get it cut on my next trip to see my father and Jassy.'

'Do you have to? Cut your hair, I mean, not visit your family.' Harry's head tilted on one side as he gave her a considering look. 'I like it curling round your ears like that.'

'Do you? I always had it cut short because—well, because Chris preferred it like that.'

'I should wear it the way *you* like best,' he advised, and changed the subject.

CHAPTER SEVEN

LATER that night Frances examined herself in the mirror on her dressing-table, twisting her head this way and that, her lips pursed as she tried to decide whether she liked her hair longer or not. She had been too preoccupied to take much notice before, beyond reminding herself to get it cut on her next weekend home. It softened the angularity of her cheekbones and chin at the new length, made her look more feminine, and she shrugged, deciding to let the glossy dark curls do their own thing for a while, and at the same time save the not inconsiderable price of a haircut. Added to which, Harry liked her hair this way, too.

Frances frowned as she got into bed. Sometimes she wondered if the events of New Year's Eve had been a dream, and the brief interlude of lovemaking one of the imaginary figments Harry had once mentioned. Of course he *had* been a little drunk that night. Perhaps he'd forgotten making love to her. She could remember, though, and very pleasant it had been. More than pleasant, if she were honest. Frances heaved herself over restlessly, and thought of Chris, wondering how he and his Isla were getting along. Like a house on fire, probably. Not that the idea hurt nearly so much now as it had at first. Harry had been right. The first painful anguish had lessened quite quickly, though she doubted whether it would have done so without the help of the work she was doing, not to mention the bonus of Harry's company. It was high time she went home again. Frances felt guilty at staying away so long, and decided to go the following weekend without fail.

Harry offered the loan of the Morris again, and Frances had an enjoyable time with Jassy and Matt, and was about to leave on the Monday morning when her father brought in the post before leaving for his office. He handed a couple of letters to Jassy and another to Frances before kissing them both and hurrying off.

'It's from Edinburgh,' said Frances with foreboding, and looked across at Jassy, who was staring in dismay at the card in her hand. Her face had lost colour, and she looked up at Frances reluctantly.

'So is this. It's a wedding invitation.'

Frances tore open her own envelope, and sure enough inside there was a gilt-lettered card from a Mr and Mrs Logan, inviting her to the marriage of their daughter, Isla Margaret, and Mr Christopher Bradley on Easter Saturday.

Jassy got up and flung her arms round Frances. 'He should have told you first,' she said fiercely.

'Hey, don't upset yourself over it.' Frances patted Jassy's smock gently. 'Or him. Don't worry, I'm fine—really.' She laughed a little and touched the card. 'Chris didn't tell me he was marrying the boss's daughter. Miss Isla Logan, no less—nice work!'

'Oh, Frances—does it hurt?'

'Well, yes, a bit. But not quite as much as I thought it would.' Frances sighed. 'I never imagined the wedding would be so soon though, Jassy.' And she put her head on her young stepmother's shoulder and let herself be comforted for a moment or two before pulling herself together to set off for Curthoys Court.

At first she was angry as she drove, thinking that Chris was being very insensitive to expect her to turn up at his wedding, but after a while she grew more rational, realising he could hardly have not invited her, either—a case of Catch Twenty-Two. Since the wedding was in Edinburgh it was too far for her father to take Jassy because of the baby, and Frances was quite certain no one would expect the old girlfriend to put in an appearance on the happy day. Too embarrassing for words.

When she arrived at the Court, Frances found it a lot less

peaceful than when she left. The ladies of the local
voluntary service had arrived in full force, as they did
every year at this time, to give Mrs Bates a helping hand to
get the house in shape for the opening, and Frances was
introduced to them all. She was surprised and very pleased
by their keen interest in her work on the archives, but
eventually excused herself to retreat to the peace and quiet
of her attic away from the hustle and bustle as the diligent
ladies, watched over by Mrs Bates, polished furniture and
silver, and dusted ornate picture frames with loving care.

Despite a pang of disappointment when she heard Harry
was away on a round of auctions, Frances was rather
grateful for the opportunity to get herself together before
he returned. Mopping her up once was permissible, but
twice would be tiresome—broken hearts tended to get
boring, unless the organ in question was one's own. Not that
broken was exactly the word for hers, Frances found; a bit
dented, perhaps, but in time she was sure it would be as
good as new if she worked on it.

Once the ladies of the WVS had vacated the premises,
Frances returned to the library to spend long hours at the
table, working hard over the descriptions intended to
accompany the books left open on display. One of her more
esoteric accomplishments was the ability to write in
manuscript similar to that of medieval monks, so with the
aid of a set of special nibs and some pots of poster paint she
was inscribing the thick white cards bought for the purpose,
hoping the result would be a pleasant surprise for Harry.
Her hand moved slowly and methodically to make the even
thick and thin strokes, the main text in cobalt blue and the
capitals ornate and embellished in crimson. She was lost to
the world, the tip of her tongue caught between her teeth,
when Mrs Bates interrupted her half-way through one
morning.

'A Mr Latimer to see you, Miss Frances,' she announced.

Frances looked up at her absently. 'To see me? Are you
sure, Mrs Bates?'

'That's what he said, dear. He's from the Astcote *Gazette*, and Mr Harry mentioned doing an article on the library and the muniment room, and told him to ask for Miss Wilding, the archivist.'

'But I thought Mr Harry was going to show him round himself!'

'Well, this Mr Latimer's here now, dear. Says he has to see you today or the article won't be out in next week's paper, and it will miss the opening of the house.'

Frances sighed, glancing down at herself. 'I'm not terribly tidy. Can he wait in the hall, or something, while I wash—I'm covered in paint.'

'He'll wait as long as you want,' said Mrs Bates loftily. 'You take your time. I'll bring coffee in a few minutes.'

Frances ran to the cloakroom near the kitchen and took off the old shirt she was using as an artist's smock. Underneath she had on her scarlet sweater, black ribbed leggings over black lacy tights, and black suede lace-up brogues, all of which would have to do. She ran a comb through her wildly untidy hair, scrubbed at her paint-stained fingers and rummaged in her bag for a lipstick to add some colour to her face before she went back along the stone-flagged passage to the great hall. A man was standing with his back to her, examining the coat of arms above the big fireplace. His hair was dark and curly like her own, but longer, he was wearing jeans and a leather waistcoat over a bright yellow shirt, and had a camera slung round his neck.

'Mr Latimer?' asked Frances, and he turned round, heavy black eyebrows rising to meet his hair as he saw the small figure in front of him.

'Are you the archivist?' he asked, patently taken aback.

'Yes. Frances Wilding. How do you do?' She held out her hand. 'Mrs Bates said you were from the Astcote *Gazette*.'

He took the hand in his, still staring at her. 'Are you really the archivist researching into the Curthoys records?'

'Yes.' Frances withdrew her hand deliberately.

'I didn't hear you were so young. I imagined tweed and

spectacles and hair screwed up in a bun.' His eyes were bold and assessing and Frances's hackles rose.

'Ah, Mrs Bates,' she said in relief as the door opened.

'Shall I take the tray into the library, Miss Frances?' Mrs Bates cast a look of disapproval at the reporter.

'Yes, please, Mrs B.'

The man sprang to relieve Mrs Bates of the tray, giving her a flashing smile. 'Allow me. That tray looks too heavy for a lady.'

His ingratiating manner cut no ice with the lady in question, and she surrendered her burden with obvious reluctance as Frances preceded the journalist from the hall.

The reporter set the tray down carefully on the covered section of the table in the library, where Frances instructed, and looked about him with avid interest. 'Is this one of the rooms being opened for the first time to the public?'

'Yes.' Frances eyed his camera curiously. 'You take your own photographs?'

'When necessary. Jack-of-all-trades, that's me.'

'Would you care for coffee?'

'Thanks. Black, one sugar.' He prowled round the room, inspecting the books and furnishings, then turned his attention to the cards Frances was lettering. 'Your work?'

She nodded. 'What exactly do you want to know, Mr Latimer?'

He leaned against the table casually, looking at her over the rim of the coffee-cup. 'Tell me about the records you're compiling.'

Frances complied, her aloof manner thawing as she described the diligently kept records of the Stuart and Parliament periods, and explaining that in the beginning these would be the main nucleus of the muniments on display. The man made swift notes as she talked, asking succinct questions which encouraged her to warm to her theme.

'This should make an interesting piece,' he said, after half an hour or so. 'Now let's have a photograph of you at the table to go with it.'

'Oh, no.' Frances stared at him in dismay. 'Mr Latimer, I'm not in the least photogenic. Besides, it should be Mr Curthoys, not me.'

'You're prettier, Miss Wilding.' He grinned and removed the tray from the table. 'Just sit down here and pick up your pen, as if you're in the middle of one of these cards.'

'Oh, but——'

He pushed her down into the chair at the table, and thrust a pen into her hand.

'All quite painless, I assure you.'

Frances seethed while he adjusted the camera. 'Mr Curthoys made no mention of any photographs of me,' she protested gruffly.

'Miss Wilding—Frances—relax!' Tony Latimer's eyes gleamed at her familiarly as he dodged to and fro, searching out the best angle. 'Now, smile—no, not like that. Think of something pleasant.'

At that moment the pleasantest thing Frances could think of was blacking the reporter's eye. She smiled at the thought, and the man had the shot he wanted.

'Perfect!' he announced jubilantly.

Something about the man's entire personality set Frances's teeth on edge, and she longed to see the back of him. 'If you've finished, Mr Latimer, I'm extremely busy, and would like to get on.'

The flashing, impertinent smile was trained on her full blast. 'Just one thing more. Harry said you'd take me along to the church to let me have a look at it.'

'Mr Curthoys said that!' Frances found it hard to believe.

'He knows old churches are a hobby of mine, and said I could have a look at this one while I was here since he's not opening it up this season.' He busied himself with his camera as he spoke. 'My special interest is in hatchments, and he says the ones on the church walls are particularly fine.'

With utmost reluctance Frances left the journalist and went to the kitchen for the necessary keys.

'Mrs B., this reporter says Mr Curthoys actually suggested I take him round the church,' she said unhappily. 'Do you think I really should?'

'I expect so dear. Mr Harry said last weekend someone would be coming from the *Gazette*, and that you'd see to him and show him round.' Mrs Bates took a bunch of keys from the row of hooks. 'Here you are, but don't be long, your lunch is nearly ready.'

'Not a moment longer than I can help. The man's held me up too long already.' Frances sighed, and went off to conduct Tony Latimer along the path to the yew-screened church.

'Interesting building,' he commented as they reached it. 'I like the embattled tower. Fifteenth century?'

'Yes.' Frances unlocked the door. 'The nave is earlier, thirteenth century, and the chancel much later, early seventeenth.' She switched on the main lights of the church and stood by the font, arms folded, while the reporter walked quickly down the aisle. As he came level with the side chapel he glanced at Frances casually.

'Any light for this part?'

Lips compressed she pressed the necessary switch, and Tony Latimer whistled, his eyes glistening. 'So that's the celebrated tomb!' He fairly leapt towards it, and Frances tore after him, almost screaming her protests as flash bulbs popped and Tony Latimer almost danced in gloating delight as he took several shots of the tomb before she could prevent him. Frances caught him by the arm, shaking with rage.

'How dare you!' she spat. 'You were supposed to look round the church, not photograph it. All that nonsense about hatchments—you haven't looked at them. This tomb was what you were after, wasn't it?' She lunged for his camera, but he laughed, eluding her easily.

'Hey, cool it, sweetheart. These shots are for my own private pleasure only. Completely off the record, I promise you. Now would I upset a local bigwig like Harry Curthoys, and me just a hack on the local rag? I'd lose my job.'

'I hope you're telling the truth,' she said icily, and jerked her head towards the door. 'Now I'll see you off the premises, Mr Latimer, if you wouldn't mind.'

'I'm going, I'm going.' He went down the aisle before her, his hands raised in mock surrender, and Frances marched after him, switching off lights and closing the door with a reverberating thud. She turned the key in the lock with finality and waved the journalist ahead of her.

'Please leave quickly, Mr Latimer. I want to make sure you've really gone before I get back to work.'

He grinned at her infuriatingly. 'Has anyone told you how cute you are when you're angry? No? I envy Harry Curthoys. Must be very pleasant having a tempting little morsel like you to whip his, er, records into shape.'

With murder in her heart Frances kept up a stony silence until she spotted Mason the gardener digging in one of the flowerbeds.

'Good afternoon, Mason,' she called. 'Would you be kind enough to show this gentleman to his car, please.'

'Right you are, Miss Frances.' Mason was elderly, but very burly, and stood six foot three in his muddy boots. He dug his fork in the ground and came towards them, brushing the dirt off his hands. 'This way, sir.'

Tony Latimer glanced at the girl's rigid face and shrugged. 'If I must, I must. Thank you for the interview— *inter alia.*'

'Goodbye,' said Frances tightly, and turned on her heel to march into the house.

She had no opportunity to confide her misgivings about the interview to Harry until the weekend, when he burst into the gatehouse early on Sunday morning while Frances was eating a solitary breakfast at the parlour table. He looked pale and tired, and his bloodshot eyes stared angrily into hers as he thrust a newspaper under her nose.

'Have you seen this?' he demanded, with no preliminaries.

Frances swallowed a mouthful of toast and eyed the paper apprehensively. 'No, I've been reading the *Sunday Times* magazine.'

'For once you may find this less exalted bit of journalism more interesting. Here.' He pushed the paper into her hand and Frances saw it was folded to the gossip column and her heart sank. Most of the column was devoted to an article by one Don Ryder, and above it were two photographs: herself, smiling dreamily across the library table, and the other was of Hal Curthoys's tomb. 'Remember Harry Curthoys?' said the caption, after which the reporter proceeded to jog the public's memory regarding the aristocratic young roisterer in his college days, his lack of money now he had inherited his estate, his abortive romance with Annabel Hayward Breckenridge, and how these days the charming unmarried scion of the Curthoys family had a pretty pet archivist under his roof to grace his muniment room, and possibly other more private rooms into the bargain. 'Rumour has it, Harry must marry,' hinted the reporter, 'to get the money Daddy left in trust. Big mystery, therefore, why the beauteous Annabel jilted our hero. Bigger still why Harry's still a bachelor. Maybe little Miss Archivist will hit the jackpot—or is there some well-hidden secret why Harry's clinging to his single status? Of course, he's always got the famous tomb to draw the crowds; remember the lady who swore Harry's ancestor got up and walked? Even I'm not sceptical now I've seen him for myself!'

Frances laid the paper down, feeling sick. One look at Harry's incensed face made her feel even worse.

'Now tell me why you let Don Ryder over the doorstep,' he ground out.

'I didn't know who he was.' Frances fought to keep her voice steady. 'Mrs Bates just said the reporter had arrived from the Astcote *Gazette*, and that you'd told her he was coming.'

'Surely you realised this wasn't the right man?'

'How was I to know? I just assumed he was the one you mentioned.'

'You assumed! Couldn't you have asked?' He flung away to stare angrily through the window. 'So how much of that—that drivel did you tell him?'

'Nothing.' Frances could feel her own temper beginning to rise. 'I merely gave him a few details about the work I'm doing.'

'No titillating details about Annabel and so on?'

'Of course not! You can't believe I'd do that! If so, why didn't I tell the man exactly how the money was left?'

'You may have done, for all I know. God knows why you didn't hand over Arabella's journal and finish the job.' he said in disgust. 'Not that a bona fide poisoning would probably be as interesting to someone like Don Ryder as the sickening innuendo he deals in. The swine even manages to infer that either I've got you in my bed as well as in my muniment room, or that Annabel threw me over because I'm bloody well gay!' He swung round, his eyes glittering at her in rage. 'And to cap it all you actually let him into the church!'

Frances sprang to her feet, stung by his injustice. 'He gave me a very convincing story about your recommending him to see it, the hatchments in particular. Then before I realised what he intended he'd begun taking photographs of the tomb. I tried to take his camera away from him, but he prevented it and promised me the shots would be off the record and he just wanted them for his own personal pleasure.'

'How could you be so bloody *gullible*? I suppose you realise now that we'll have hordes of people queuing up to get in here, all thirsting to see that blasted tomb again—not

to mention wanting a look at me! Or you.' Harry's nostrils
flared with distaste. 'I might as well open the church
officially again—no point in keeping it locked now.
Perhaps I could put a notice up "Visitors of a nervous
disposition are not advised to enter". That should do the
trick. They'll be stampeding to get in. I could charge
extra—might even take enough to pay for a few square feet
of lead roof!'

'I had no idea the man was from a national paper,' said
Frances in desperation. 'I honestly believed I was just
giving the local *Gazette* a few facts about the archives, as we
agreed.' She struck the paper viciously. 'This man hasn't
used one word of the information I gave him. All he wanted
was the photographs.'

Harry shrugged coldly. 'Whatever you did or said makes
no difference now. The result is there in black and white in
newsprint, which far too many people take for the gospel
truth, you naïve little fool.'

Frances went white. 'I shall leave here at once, of course,'
she said proudly.

There was a sudden, appalled silence in the room. It was
only by sheer willpower that Frances kept her eyes steady
as she stared in defiance at Harry, who looked for a moment
as though she had dealt him a blow in the stomach. Then
his head went up and he stared down his prominent nose at
her, his face as deathly pale as hers.

'No way,' he said with violence. 'I demand a month's
notice at least so that you can finish some of the work you
came here to do.'

Frances felt sick inside. 'Just as you wish, of course. Now
if you'll just stand aside I'll get over to the library and put
the finishing touches to the items going on display. After
that I'll be able to work in the attic all the time until I leave.'
And keep as far out of your way as I possibly can, she added
silently.

'Very well.' The hostility on Harry's face transformed
him into a stranger as he swung round and strode from the

room without another word.

Frances sat down limply, utterly bowled over by the fact that Harry's easy-going, casual charm was very deceptive, and hid an unsuspected, rock-hard core beneath. Where had his sense of humour been this morning? Not to mention the sense of fair play his expensive school was supposed to have drummed into him, she thought, smarting with injustice. Men! Frances gave an inelegant snort. Who needed them? After all, if her life-long chum tore off after the first pretty girl he met in his new job, why should she be fool enough to expect any special consideration from Harry Curthoys, who had known her for a mere month or two. And as for that vile reporter—Matt Wilding would have been startled to hear some of the words used by his daughter to vent her wrath on the head of the unsuspecting Don Ryder. Grinding her teeth in impotent fury, she tried to comfort herself with the thought that there was still her work to fall back on. As she had learned over the past few months, it was a very effective anodyne for hurt feelings. And she *was* hurt. She liked Harry. Or had. Now it would be difficult to go on working here under the circumstances. Nevertheless he apparently considered she owed it to him, and of course she did. He'd been very kind to her in so many ways, which only made his blind, unreasoning reaction to the newspaper article all the more shattering when her part in it had been entirely innocent. Stupid, admittedly, but innocent just the same.

During the morning Frances completed the manuscript resumés she'd been working on, and set them out alongside the relevant books not only on the library table, but in the muniment room along with the archives. There were manuals on hawking and land tenure, a handbook on the law, a copy of a guide to the posts called *The Carrier's Cosmography*, by a man called Taylor, and her own particular favourite, a joke book entitled *The Merry Jests of the Cobbler of Canterbury*. Jokes she could use, thought Frances dispiritedly, and packed up her pens and pots of paint.

Everything was now in readiness for Good Friday, the day of the opening, and she heaved a sigh of relief, thankful that she could now retreat to the attics for the remainder of her time at Curthoys Court, and stay there, like Rochester's mad wife in *Jane Eyre*. It occurred to her that there would have to be a new arrangement about meals, too, and she went off to the kitchen to talk to Mrs Bates and ask if in future she could eat her dinner every night at the gatehouse.

'I shall be going home at weekends from now on, Mrs B.,' added Frances, trying to sound brisk, 'but if you and your husband want some peace and quiet during week nights I can easily have my dinner on a tray in my room in the evenings.'

'Miss Frances!' Mrs Bates stopped beating cake mixture in a basin and stared at the strained face of the girl. 'Whatever's wrong? I saw Mr Harry storming off this morning and you left most of your lunch. What's he been saying to you?'

It seemed best to explain to her about the reporter and his scurrilous behaviour; then Frances fetched the *Sunday Post* for Mrs Bates to read. 'Mr Curthoys blames me for all that,' she said sadly. 'I wanted to leave right away, but he considers I owe him a month's notice, so I'll work up in the attic until then. There's more room up there now, and the weather's warmer.'

'Mr Harry has a bad temper, but he rarely loses it these days. I'm sure he didn't mean to upset you,' said Mrs Bates, worried.

'Then I hope never to see him when he *does* mean it,' said Frances with a wry smile. 'Anyway, I won't be dining over here any more. I think I'll go for a stroll in the park now—it's quite pleasant outside. Then I'll go back to the gatehouse, Mrs B. I won't start anything new today.'

'But what about your tea?'

'I'm not hungry, thanks. I'll make myself a cup in the gatehouse when I get back.'

Frances collected a windbreaker from her bedroom and went out to walk briskly in the rather pale sunshine. There was a stiff breeze and she ducked her head into it and forged along at a rapid pace, trying to keep her mind blank as the exercise sent the blood glowing along her veins. But she couldn't help wondering where Harry was spending the afternoon, since he was usually home by this time on Sundays. Wherever he was it was nothing to do with her, she reminded herself, and jogged back to the gatehouse to make her Sunday call home, which was more prolonged than usual, since her father had read the article in the paper, and was very uptight about the inferences regarding his only daughter.

'Maybe you'll have another one soon,' said Frances, in an attempt to divert him.

'Not yet. Jassy had a scan on Friday and not only is Baby Wilding doing well at this stage, we actually know he's a boy!'

'Amazing—the things they can do these days!'

The happy news succeeded in diverting Matt from threats to sue the *Sunday Post*, to Frances's relief, and she rang off before he could bring up the emotive subject of how Harry was taking it.

After an hour in the bath with a book, Frances felt disinclined to get dressed up for the sole purpose of eating her dinner off a tray in her room. Since the Bateses were going to evening service in the village church she would be on her own for the evening, and decided to get into her pyjamas and catch up on some correspondence in bed until it was time to eat. She was scribbling away to Caroline Napier when the door banged downstairs and Harry's voice shouted up the stairs. 'Frances? Are you up there?'

She sat rigid against the pillows, willing him to go away.

'Frances?' he yelled again, then to her dismay he came up the stairs two at a time and knocked on her door and threw it open.

'Why didn't you answer me?' he demanded, standing in the open doorway.

Frances slid under the bedclothes, her face hostile. 'I hoped you'd go away,' she said bluntly.

Harry looked at her, contrition in the narrow grey eyes. 'I've come to apologise. Grovel. Anything to make up for the way I went for you this morning.' He ran a hand through his hair distractedly. 'I read the article, went up like a rocket and dashed over here to take it out on you in sheer bloody-mindedness. I'm sorry. Deeply sorry. When I got to Astcote this morning I rang Tony Latimer—the genuine article—and he told me some flashy chap was in his place this week saying he was a free-lance photographer keen on taking some shots of local scenery, including some of the Court. He lured one of the typists out for a drink and no doubt was well primed with information by the time he got to you.'

Frances merely stared at him in stony silence.

'I know what you're thinking,' he said heavily. 'I should have believed you without needing confirmation from someone else.'

'Something like that.'

'Dolly gave me a right dressing-down when I came home,' he went on morosely. 'Told me how you had to be persuaded to see the swine at all, and how worried you were about taking him to the church—all of which I should have known perfectly well.' His face looked bleak. 'It was just that I was so poleaxed when I saw your face smiling at me from that damn rag, well, I just hit out in reaction to that poisonous rubbish about our relationship.'

'Whereas we're just good friends,' she said without emotion. 'Or were.'

Harry winced. 'I'd like to think we still are—if you can manage to overlook the scene I made this morning, that is.'

After her day of utter misery Frances found she wasn't noble enough for that yet. 'I'll try,' she said non-committally.

'Does that mean you're willing to come over to the house to dinner tonight?'

'No, I don't think so.'

Harry stood very erect. 'You mean I've put myself beyond the pale,' he said very quietly.

'I just think it's better if we stick to our proper places in future. Yours is over there.' Frances waved a hand towards the window overlooking the Court. 'Mine, for a little while, is here, until I finish the job you're paying me to do.'

Harry's mouth compressed. 'I hurt you very badly, didn't I? It's this blasted temper of mine. I've learned to control it pretty well these last few years, but just once in a while it breaks loose and gets the better of me.'

'It doesn't matter,' she said coolly. 'But for a moment this morning I felt like a serf with my neck under the heel of the overlord.'

He breathed in sharply. 'That's hitting below the belt!'

'Possibly. But it's how I felt. And as I have no intention of ever putting myself in that position again I'll keep to my side of the fence in future.'

'I see,' Harry's eyes locked with hers for several moments, then he gave an odd, formal little bow and left, closing the door behind him with great care.

Frances lay with hands clenched until she heard him leave the house, then she indulged in a few relieving tears, blew her nose hard and resumed her letter-writing. She was so successful in her determination to carry on with her task she was deep in her third letter when she became aware of much coming and going below stairs. Eventually the Bateses could be heard upstairs getting ready for church, then Mrs Bates popped her head, in its best hat, round the door and informed Frances her dinner was in the oven and would be ready in about five minutes. Would she mind fetching it herself, and they would see her later. Frances decided to finish her letter, and it was a good fifteen minutes afterwards when she heard footsteps on the stairs again. Her blood ran cold at the thought that it was dark now, and anyone could have come in unnoticed if the Bateses had forgotten to lock the door. Her heart was in her mouth as the bedroom door began to open gradually, then her colour came back in a great tide as Harry, now in a light blue jersey and elderly jeans, backed slowly into the room bearing an enormous wooden tray. Without a word he placed it very carefully on the dressing-table, then turned to a goggling Frances and flicked out a starched white napkin with a flourish.

'Allow me, madam,' he said, poker-faced, and plumped up the pillows behind her before spreading the napkin over the duvet.

'What on earth do you imagine you're doing?' demanded Frances irritably.

'Role reversal. Now I'm the serf and you have the upper hand,' he informed her and whisked away to fetch a plate arranged with vegetables, roast pheasant and game chips. He set it before her with a flourish, handing her a knife and fork.

'But I can't——'

'Yes, you can,' he contradicted. 'There's only one catch—I'm going to sit on the end of your bed and eat mine with you. Not exactly serflike, I'm afraid, but I'm starving, and you must be too. Dolly said you left your lunch and didn't have any tea.' He began to eat with concentration and waved at her to do the same. Frances stared at him helplessly then shrugged in defeat and began to eat, largely because she found she was just as hungry as Harry.

'Does Mrs Bates know you're doing this?' she asked indistinctly.

'Sort of.'

'What do you mean—sort of?'

'She was under the impression we were going to eat downstairs,'

'Then why are we eating up here?'

'I though I'd never *get* you downstairs in the mood you were in earlier, and as I was fading fast from malnutrition I took the war into the enemy's camp, so to speak.' Harry paused, fork half-way to his mouth, and looked at her. 'Only I'd much rather we weren't enemies, Frances.'

Suddenly the ridiculous aspect of their situation struck Frances and she choked with laughter, then began to splutter as a morsel of food went down the wrong way. Harry jumped to his feet to dump his plate on the tray, then rescued hers. He thumped her on the back until she could breathe again and beg for mercy, eyes streaming. When order was restored and they had resumed eating, Frances asked how on earth the dinner had managed to travel so far and stay so hot.

'I bought Dolly a microwave. Had the chance of one going cheap. I brought it over this evening, plugged it in and *voilà*, two hot dinners. Couldn't manage serving dishes and all that, though. Had to put it all on the plate and hope for the best.' He grinned at her. 'Good job that skunk Ryder can't see us now.'

Frances chuckled as she waved a hand at her blue and white striped pyjamas. 'Not really *femme fatale* gear, Harry.'

Harry gave her a rather wry smile. 'I'm not sure I agree with you there, somehow, Frances Wilding. You look pretty fetching to me.'

She handed him her plate, flushing a little. 'I really don't know why I'm having dinner in bed like an invalid anyway. I was about to get up when your fairy footsteps frightened the life out of me.'

'Why *were* you in bed, Frances? Were you feeling ill?'

She looked away. 'No. I went for a walk when I finished in the library, then I had a bath, and suddenly it seemed like too much trouble to get dressed so I crawled in here, To lick my wounds, if I'm honest.'

Harry flinched. 'The ones I inflicted.'

Frances nodded, not trying to contradict what was only the truth. 'But now I'd better get up before Mr and Mrs Bates get back. I don't want to offend them.'

'There's a gateau thing here, or cheese and biscuits, but I

haven't made coffee yet.'

'Let's eat the rest downstairs. I feel an utter fraud lying here.'

Harry opened the door and collected the tray. 'Will you come over to the house to drink coffee? Please?'

Since they'd had dinner together, and in her bedroom at that, Frances saw little point in refusing. 'Yes,' she said after a moment's thought.

'Thank you.' He smiled at her, looking gratifyingly relieved, and went downstairs with the tray.

Frances jumped out of bed and dressed hurriedly in her crimson wool dress, dragging a comb through her hair at top speed. Her shining eyes and pink cheeks came as rather a surprise when she saw her reflection in the mirror—a very different apparition from the wan creature that had stared back at her before she got into bed.

CHAPTER EIGHT

LATER, when they were lounging either side of the morning-room fire after praline gateau and coffee, Frances could almost have imagined the episode of the morning had never happened, and said so idly.

'I wish it hadn't,' Harry said with feeling. 'Put it down to temporary malfunction of the grey cells. It pulled me up pretty sharp when you talked about leaving, though.'

'Afraid you wouldn't find someone else willing to work up in the attic?' she asked teasingly.

'No. Not quite. I—well, let's say it brought to life a seed that had been about to germinate in my brain for some time.' He took in a deep breath. 'Frances, I want you to listen carefully. Hear me out.'

Frances stiffened. Harry's profile was outlined sharply by the flickering firelight, which emphasised the hollows beneath his cheekbones as he lay in a half-reclining position in the tapestry-covered chair. One of his hands rested on the arm, and Frances kept her eyes on the long, slim fingers and the heavy signet ring that threw back red-gold gleams as the flames caught it. 'I'm listening,' she said quietly.

'Frances, are you still yearning for your lost love?' he asked, surprisingly.

'It wouldn't do much good if I were. He's getting married on Easter Saturday.'

Harry straightened, staring at her. 'That's a bit quick. When did you find out?'

'At home last weekend. I received an invitation.'

'Were you shattered by the news?'

She shrugged philosophically. 'A little. But I've got used to the idea now. I shan't go to the wedding though.'

There was silence in the room for a while, then Harry

cleared pretty sharpish his throat rather noisily. 'Frances, you know most of what there is to know about me—including the rotten temper you came up against this morning. You know I need to marry, and you know the terms of the will, and you know how desperately I need money.'

Frances sat very still, her eyes wide as she gazed at Harry's tense face.

'I think you know what I'm about to say,' he went on jerkily. 'This morning, when you said you were leaving right away, I was shattered. My temper braked to a grinding halt. Believe me, the red mist cleared only I just couldn't seem to express myself very gracefully at the time! I've grown used to having you around, Frances. Hell—you may not recognise it as such, but what I'm struggling to get out is a proposal.' He raised a hand as Frances opened her mouth to speak. 'Now I know very well you don't love me, but I hope in time you could at least grow fond of me. Just as—as fond as I am of you. We get on well together, share a lot of the same interests, and you said you liked children. Because, of course, that's the snag, I'm afraid. I mean, would you be willing to have a shot at giving me a son? From my own personal point of view I'd be more than happy to have a daughter, anyway, but as you already know, an heir would make life a lot easier all round. God knows, I've no aversion to hard work, but I just can't find a way of earning enough to keep this place going indefinitely.' Harry came to a halt, giving her a hunted look. 'Lord, this is a hellishly unromantic sort of proposal.' He turned away to stare into the fire, making no request for an immediate answer. Frances was very grateful, since for the time being she seemed to have been struck dumb.

'You're very young,' went on Harry heavily after a while, still not looking at her. 'Probably the thought of tying yourself down to a virtual stranger with a view to getting pregnant as quickly as you can doesn't sound like a very attractive proposition.'

Frances considered the idea objectively. The right job had been very hard to find since she graduated, and there was a great gap left in her life by Chris's defection. One way and another marriage to Harry Curthoys could be the solution to everything and, if she were entirely honest, by no means as unattractive a prospect as he seemed to think.

'You've taken me by surprise, to say the least,' she said after a lengthy pause. 'I never imagined——'

'At least you didn't come out with a straight no!' Harry twisted in his chair to smile at her whimsically.

'Very true. Look, would you mind if I had a little time to think about it?'

'As much as you want. Talk it over with your family, if you like.'

'No, I don't need to do that. This would have to be my own decision.' Frances put her head on one side and gave him a funny little smile. 'Besides—from a father's point of view you're a very good catch for any girl.'

Harry gave a wry laugh, 'I don't know about that. Anyway,' he jumped to his feet, 'let's have a drink. Brandy, Frances?'

'Last time I drank that I fell asleep on your lap!'

'Why do you think I suggested it?' he said promptly. 'I think you were wearing the same dress, too.'

'So I was.' She hesitated. 'I'd like some brandy if there's some ginger ale to mix with it.'

'Certainly, madam.'

'No good, Harry, I just can't see you as a waiter.'

'Why not?'

'You look exactly what you are.'

'I don't think I'm going to like it, but tell me what I am anyway.'

'You look like Harry Curthoys of Curthoys Court, even when you're dressed in denims, or stoned out of your mind.' Frances smiled cheekily as she took her drink from him. 'Blood will tell, as they say.'

Harry grimaced as he poured himself two fingers of

single malt whisky from the bottle Charlotte had given him.

'If you're right I may have a drop or two of Arabella's in my veins, which will do me no good. You'd hardly fancy marrying a man with murder in his genes.'

'No problem. Things are different now. If you wanted to get rid of me you wouldn't have to resort to poison, you could just divorce me for non-fulfilment of my conjugal duties, or physical cruelty, or whatever else might have turned you off me.' Her eyes sparkled with mischief over her glass and he laughed as he sat down again.

'How long will you need to come to a decision?' Harry asked presently.

Frances regarded him directly. 'There are one or two points I'd like to clarify before I make up my mind.'

'What, exactly?'

'Say I produced a girl each time I became pregnant, supposing I were willing to go on trying for a boy,' she began practically. 'You'd be worse off than ever. No money and even more mouths to feed.'

'Perhaps I didn't make myself clear,' he said quietly. 'I meant you need try only once. You could have a divorce after that if you liked—I mean, if you had a girl and didn't fancy another try.'

'Oh, yes, and what about the child? Do I just pop off and leave my daughter with you?' Frances fixed him with a very challenging look, and Harry spread his hands, sighing.

'Sorry. I'm not thinking straight after the incident this morning. All I know is that when you said you were leaving it felt like an ice-pack thrown in my face.' He smiled at her. 'If you go, Frances, I'll be losing the greatest source of comfort I've had in my life for a long time.'

'Comfort!' She giggled. 'You make me sound like an old shoe—quite a compliment.'

Harry got to his feet and began prowling round the room. 'From my point of view it is a compliment. I am comfortable and relaxed with you around. You're such a restful creature, Frances, nothing frenetic or restless about you. Not like Annabel, who was always on the go, needing parties and theatres and nightclubs which I just couldn't afford, in money or energy.'

'But physically she turned you on,' put in Frances.

Harry stopped his prowling, 'Yes. She did. She's very beautiful. I missed her badly when she took off so abruptly.'

Frances nodded thoughtfully. 'In bed, you mean.'

He turned away, frowning. 'Yes. We were very compatible in that way, at least.' Swiftly he came to crouch beside her chair and gather her hand in his. 'Frances, if you have reservations about that side of marriage I wouldn't trouble you more than absolutely necessary. I mean we could go on being good friends just as we are now, only we'd be obliged to share a bed now and then—for obvious reasons.'

'And you'd be saved the expense of my salary, too,' she teased.

'My God! You don't think that has anything to do with it?'

'No, no, of course not.' She laughed and touched his hand lightly. 'Now, I'm going to finish my drink and you can escort me back to the gatehouse, and I'll sleep on the idea.'

Harry leapt to his feet in one graceful movement. 'When will you give me your answer?'

'Are you home to dinner tomorrow night?'

'I'll make a point of it.' He hesitated, fixing her with a rather unsettling look. 'But there is one thing I feel I must stipulate, even though it may influence your decision. I know you were hit very hard when this man of yours found someone else, and I'm fully aware of the efforts you've made to get over him. I want you to be my wife very much, but make no mistake, Frances, I'd rather you turned me down if you can't get Chris out of your mind. No man wants a wife who yearns for some other chap, particularly at, well, certain private moments.'

'You mean, when making love.'

'Absolutely. I'm only human. I promise never to hanker after Annabel again if you marry me, on condition that for you it's the same with regard to Chris.' Harry's eyes held hers very steadily. 'Is what I'm asking impossible?'

Frances returned his gaze unwaveringly. 'I'll think about it, and if I find that it is I shall say no, I promise.' She drained her glass and stood up, suddenly feeling weary. 'It's been quite a day, one way or another. I think I'll go to bed.'

'Back to bed, you mean.' Harry chuckled as he helped her on with her coat.

'I hope I'm left in more peace this time than I was earlier on!'

'Oh, come on! How many people get dinner served to them in bed?'

'Especially by Harry Curthoys!'

'On the last point only you, Frances Wilding.' Harry took her hand in his as they went through the dimly lit house, and when they reached the entrance hall he stopped and turned her to face him. 'If your answer is no tomorrow night I shall never feel entitled to ask for a kiss again. So while we're still in a sort of no man's land shall we kiss and make up properly?'

Frances looked up at him consideringly for a moment, then held up her face. He drew her to him, but instead of kissing her he laid his cheek on her hair and held her tightly.

'I'm sorry I hurt you, Frances,' he murmured. 'Have you really forgiven me for getting the wrong end of the stick?'

She nodded, her face buried against his sweater, liking the feel of it, and liking the scent of him too. No overpowering aura of aftershave or cologne for Harry; he smelt of expensive soap and fresh air, with the faintest hint of whisky.

'Say it then,' he ordered, and she raised her head, smiling at him.

'Yes, I have. We won't talk about it any more. Let's

forget about it entirely, only you might cancel delivery of the *Sunday Post* as a gesture.'

'Done,' he said, laughing, and kissed her smiling mouth. He raised his head a little to look into her eyes then held her closer and kissed her again. Frances relaxed against him involuntarily, responding in a way that sent tremors through Harry's body.

'Come back to the fire,' he said unsteadily after a while, and Frances came down to earth.

'Once was an accident,' she said, breathless, and gave a husky little gurgle. 'If Bates found you asleep in a chair in the morning again it could be a bit hard to explain, especially if I were still on your lap this time.'

Harry grinned wickedly. 'You'd have to marry me then—you'd be compromised!'

'People don't get compromised any more.' Frances laughed and made for the door. 'Now, are you escorting me back or shall I sprint across the courtyard on my own? I don't mind.'

'*I* do.' Harry banged the outer door behind him and took her by the hand, glancing up at the sky. 'That moon's fairly new—shall we make a wish?'

They stood hand in hand, staring up at the moon in silence, then resumed their walk.

'What did you wish for Frances?'

'One mustn't tell, or it won't come true.'

'Then mum's the word,' he said promptly. 'Because I want mine to come true more than anything I've wanted in a long time.'

'Except Annabel?'

'It's bad form to keep throwing up a chap's past at him,' he said severely.

'Yes, sir, sorry, sir.' Frances tugged at the curls on her forehead, and bobbed him a curtsey as they reached the gatehouse. 'Beg pardon, your honour, won't happen again——'

'Wretch!' Harry grabbed her and shook her hard, much

to Mrs Bates's disapproval when she opened the door to them.

'Mr Harry! What *are* you doing? Let Miss Frances go at once!'

'Yes, Dolly,' said Harry, grinning, and stood back, giving Frances an outrageous wink. 'Goodnight, Frances. Goodnight, Dolly.'

As the two women bade him goodnight Harry turned to go back to the Court, then he glanced at Frances, his face abruptly serious.

'Tomorrow night, then, Frances.'

She nodded gravely, and went indoors with a curious Mrs Bates, smiling at her reassuringly. 'Mr Harry's persuaded me to revert to having dinner with him again when he's home in the evenings.'

'And a very good thing, too.' Mrs Bates was plainly relieved, and shooed her lodger upstairs with promises of a hot drink once she was in bed.

Frances was glad of the soothing hot chocolate as she sat propped against her pillows, thinking hard. Did she really want to be Harry's wife? The answer to that was relatively easy. It would be no difficult task to become fond of Harry. Very fond indeed. In fact, if she were honest, she already was. But was she fond enough to rush into motherhood quite so precipitately? That was the burning question. And there was Harry's stipulation too, which was fair enough. No man wanted a wife who was mooning after someone else, however platonic the marriage might be. After thinking it over Frances came to the rather surprising conclusion that in Harry's company lately she seldom thought of Chris at all. Admittedly there were times still when she missed Chris badly, but only when she was alone, and not all the time then. The discovery made her feel guilty. In only a few months she seemed to have grown used to being without Chris far more easily than she would ever have believed possible, and it was pretty obvious that Harry Curthoys had figured largely in her recovery.

Thoughts of Harry and his proposal occupied Frances far into the night despite her weariness. It wasn't every day one received a proposal of marriage, and she felt strongly that her first merited a fair amount of attention. Chris had never asked her in so many words. She had just taken it for granted that they would marry one day. Yet he had popped the question promptly enough to his Isla, thought Frances bleakly, which was a fair indication that he had never really been in love with herself at all. Fond of her, certainly. She bit her lip, her eyes narrowed. Harry had used the word fond, too. It would be marvellous to have someone desperately in love with her for a change, in place of all this lukewarm, comfortable affection she seemed to inspire in the opposite sex. Not that there had been much of the lukewarm about Harry's kisses tonight. On the contrary. The chemistry had been just the same as on New Year's Eve, instantaneous and intense for the few moments their lips and bodies had been in contact. If she needed a deciding factor to give Harry an answer, perhaps this same chemistry was the one. Finally, Frances settled down to sleep, confident that after a night's rest she would know what to say, one way or another, the moment she woke in the morning.

'Well?' demanded Harry the following evening. He pulled Frances into the morning-room when she arrived for dinner, and closed the door behind her. She was rather touched to see that he was dressed much less casually than usual on their evenings together, in a tan, checked jacket new to her, with his thick, ash-fair hair smooth for once, in contrast to his face, which was set in tense, anxious lines. It was impossible not to feel gratified, yet Frances found it hard to come out with her answer in cold blood. She smiled at him a little diffidently as he took her jacket.

'Could we talk a little?' she asked. 'Clear up a few points first?'

Harry turned away at once to pour sherry. 'Does this

mean you have cold feet about it all—were my terms a bit off-putting?'

'Not really.' Frances accepted her glass and sipped a little before going on. 'Harry, you spoke last night of divorce, if ever I wanted it.'

'Yes.' He sat on the edge of the chair opposite and looked at her intently. 'I meant it, I would release you any time you wished if things didn't work out.'

'But you seemed to assume that once we were married and had—had cohabited, pregnancy would automatically follow. It doesn't for everyone, you know. I might not be able to deliver the goods, to be crude.' Frances stared down into her glass, unable to meet his eyes.

'Frances,' he answered quietly. 'We have no way of knowing for certain whether we will have children together if we marry. But personally I'm sure of it. Why shouldn't we? We're both healthy, normal human beings.' He rose and pulled her out of her chair, holding her hands in his. 'So give me a straight answer, Frances. Is it yes or no?'

Frances met his eyes squarely. 'As long as you're going into this with your eyes open, Harry, then it's yes.'

His grasp tightened. 'And Chris? He's not likely to form a shadowy third in a *ménage à trois* in our household when you marry me?'

'No, Harry, I promise. I'd be lying if I said he didn't still mean something to me—I've known him too long for that,' she said candidly. 'But from now on, as far as I'm concerned, he's just an old friend who's someone else's property. So if you still want me I shall be very honoured to marry you.'

Harry looked long and hard into her eyes, then smiled and held her close. 'When?' he demanded. 'How soon?'

'I don't know,' she said breathlessly. 'I hadn't got that far.'

Harry snatched up their glasses and proposed a toast. 'To us, Frances. To our mutual happiness.'

'To us,' echoed Frances smiling, and drank with him, infected by his soaring spirits.

'Oh, Frances.' He pulled her into his arms. 'Thank you. I'm very conscious of my good fortune.'

'Talking of fortunes, I'll do my best to increase yours for you.'

'Ours, Frances, ours! And at this moment I don't care two hoots about any of that. It's enough to know I'm going to have you by my side to help fight for this place.' Harry checked suddenly. 'You *do* care for the house, don't you, Frances. Understand how I feel?'

'Yes, Harry.' She gave him a whimsical smile. 'Though if I were the jealous type I fancy it's not the fair Annabel I'd be worrying about—it's Curthoys Court!'

Harry laughed and took her in his arms again. 'Ah, but I can't kiss and cuddle a house, Frances. In that area you win hands down.' And he picked her up and sat down with her on his lap and proceeded to kiss her so single-mindedly neither of them saw the door open or heard the rumble of the dinner trolley as Mrs Bates wheeled it in.

'Mr Harry!' she exclaimed, scandalised.

Harry stood Frances on her feet, laughing at her scarlet face, then gave his old nurse a hug. 'Congratulate us, Dolly—we're going to be married.'

And a month later they were, though sometimes during the weeks beforehand Frances was quite sure nothing would be ready on time. Curthoys Court was opened to the public on Good Friday, as planned, the church included, since Harry had decided to take advantage of Don Ryder's unsolicited publicity and reap some benefit from it. Before that there was the family get-together when Charlotte, Harry's sister, and her husband, James Colville, plus Matt and Jassy, came for the weekend, and Harry invited a few local friends in for drinks on the Sunday to meet the bride and her family.

Charlotte Colville was an older, feminine version of Harry, to Frances's relief, and very pleased about the wedding. 'About time the poor old darling had someone nice to keep him company in this place,' she declared, and hauled Harry and Frances off to the telephone to ring their mother in the States, resulting in a disjointed, happy conversation with Nadine Bancroft, who was unashamedly wild with excitement over the news, and promised to be at the Court well in time for the big day.

The conversation over the dinner table between them all that weekend was a lively, animated affair, with everyone getting on very well with each other, particularly after consumption of the very fine burgundy James had brought as a present for the occasion.

'Are you wearing white?' Charlotte asked Frances at one stage.

'Of course,' said Harry promptly, and turned gratefully to Matt Wilding. 'It's very good of you, sir, to let us have the ceremony here instead of in Warwickshire with you.'

Matt smiled at his daughter's glowing, happy face, 'It would have been rather a shame to deprive your people locally of a Curthoys wedding. Besides, I know Frances prefers it this way.'

'Indeed I do,' she agreed, and cast a mischievous glance at her husband-to-be. 'Particularly since I coaxed Harry to let us have the ceremony in the family church.'

James Colville chuckled. 'Pity you couldn't sell tickets, Harry, with a bride and that famous tomb for attractions.'

'James has no romance in his soul,' said his wife sadly, and leaned towards Jassy. 'The date won't clash with *your* big day, I hope?'

'No, no—it's weeks before his nibs is due to put in an appearance,' Jassy laughed. 'My main problem will be finding some kind of designer silk tent to wear; I'm getting rounder by the day!'

Frances and Jassy did their shopping together, armed with the money Matt gave his daughter for a wedding present, since she was moving into a house where literally nothing was necessary in the way of furnishings and ornaments to start her new life. Frances had never had so much to spend at one time in her life before, but even so chose her trousseau with great care, with an eye to practicability in the future. Even her wedding dress was not the fairy-tale confection her father had in mind, as the frilled taffeta creations offered to Frances just didn't suit her.

'Need to be tall, Jassy,' she sighed, and tried on ivory organza instead. Ankle-length, with a floating skirt hemmed with satin ribbon and a tucked satin sash for her slender waist, the dress had a matching hat in stiffened organza, its wide brim satin-bound like the dress.

Enthroned in a gilt chair to watch as Frances tried on the dresses offered to them, Jassy gave a sigh of bliss as she saw the last one. 'Don't try any more, darling, that's the one.'

Afterwards, over lunch, Frances asked Jassy how Mrs Bradley, Chris's mother, had reacted to the invitation.

'Convinced you're marrying Harry on the rebound!' Jassy looked at Frances anxiously. 'Are you?'

'No,' answered Frances calmly.

'Do you love him?'

'I'm very fond of him.'

'Fond!' Jassy frowned. 'Fond's not much good in bed, love.'

Frances shook her head reprovingly. 'I'm not at all sure you should be saying such things to me, Mrs Wilding. Anyway, I'm fairly sure things will be quite all right in that department, if you're really worried.'

'You mean you've been to bed with him already.'

'No, I haven't! But—how can I explain——'

'When he kisses you it's pretty obvious he'll be an effective lover,' suggested Jassy.

Frances looked at her absently, suddenly aware that the time for finding out was fairly close at hand. 'One way and another I sincerely hope so,' she said cryptically.

Once Curthoys Court was open to the public, life altered.

Despite vigorous protests from Harry, Frances retreated to the attic on open days, and only emerged again after the last visitor had gone. Easter was very warm and sunny for once, and the field which doubled as car park was full of cars for the entire holiday period. Whether it was due to the wedding announcement, the piece in Don Ryder's column, or the fact that the church was once again open to the public, wasn't clear but the net results were very satisfying. The tea shop in the stables did a roaring trade selling Mrs Bates's scones and cinnamon buns, and Frances occupied herself on the day of Chris's wedding by giving a hand in there, and managed to avoid thinking about the ceremony in Edinburgh quite successfully.

'If the crowds keep coming at this rate I might get my new roof without any help from my father's money,' said Harry one evening.

'Then you wouldn't need to marry me,' said Frances promptly.

Harry looked at her consideringly. 'Oh, I don't know, I've rather got used to the idea now. Besides, my mother arrives in a few days, and she'll give me hell if she gets home to another cancelled wedding.'

Frances winced secretly. 'Mm. A bit repetitious.'

Harry put a hand on hers, all the teasing over. 'Do *you* want to back out? There's still time.'

'No.'

'Neither do I. So stop making silly suggestions!'

Frances would have liked something a lot more romantic in the way of reassurance, but Harry instantly reverted to his usual bantering self, and made no further attempts at any lovemaking, either, beyond a kiss each night before he took her back to the gatehouse. Sometimes their relationship seemed much too platonic to have any great chance of success as a marriage, in Frances's opinion, though common sense told her it was better to have friendship as a basis than mere physical attraction with nothing to fall back on once the first heat of passion fizzled out. Nevertheless just a fraction more heat and passion would have been reassuring.

CHAPTER NINE

AFTERWARDS, whenever Frances looked back on her wedding day, it always seemed to pass in a happy, dreamlike sequence of events, seen through a golden haze like a Zefferelli film. The service itself was at noon, in a church transformed by the masses of spring flowers gathered from the gardens and parkland of Curthoys Court. March sunshine poured radiance through the windows, adding lustre to the bright gold of the daffodils and seeking out the white glimmer of Hal Curthoys in his secluded corner. But on this day of days, Frances had no thoughts to spare for the past. All her concentration was focused on the warm clasp of Harry's hand on hers and the solemn, awesome vows they made to each other before the altar. When the moment came for Harry to promise to love, honour and cherish her his fingers tightened on hers and she looked up at him, her heart missing a beat as there was a moment of utter silence before Harry began to repeat the ancient words.

His face lost some of its colour, and the look in his eyes made her tremble as his voice altered, deepened and grew husky as he made his commitment to her with a deliberation that rendered the vows Frances made in response all but inaudible as she took Harry for her husband. The rest of the service passed in a daze, not even the flurry of kissing and congratulating in the vestry as they signed the register doing much to penetrate the spell that seemed to hold her in thrall as she tried to solve the mystery of that moment when she and Harry had looked at each other in some kind of recognition that she was at a loss to define.

The couple were watched by a congregation which packed the church to capacity, while still more crowds of people from the village waited outside to greet the newly married pair as they emerged into the spring sunshine. Harry, now the ceremony was over, was plainly jubilant and waved his top hat to them all, his face alight with the well-known smile as he led his bride through the throngs of well-wishers on the way back to the house.

As they reached the inner court to wait for the rest of the wedding party to catch up, Harry's first words to his new bride were unexpectedly prosaic. 'Are those shoes up to a hike like this, Frances?'

She blinked, looking down at the fragile satin slippers, still slightly dazed by the experience in church. 'I don't suppose they are—but they're rather pretty, don't you think?'

'Exquisite—like the rest of you.' Harry's eyes were dancing as they rested on his new bride. 'But I'm not convinced I shouldn't have given you a piggy-back on the way home, just the same!'

The ancient, time-worn beauty of the house provided the perfect background as the couple posed for the wedding photographs in the obliging sunshine, and the following day most of the national newspapers carried a picture of the tall, fair-haired groom laughing down at his small bride in her charmingly simple dress and hat, a single ivory rose held in her gloved hand. When the photo session was over Harry delighted the onlookers enormously by picking Frances up and carrying her into the house to the great hall to take up their positions before the fireplace to receive their guests, and Frances was kissed and congratulated until her colour was bright from all the attention. But even so, some inner part of her was still unable to take in the fact that she really was the wife of Henry George St John Curthoys, and had promised to love and cherish him for the rest of her life.

But one thing Frances was very aware of was that she was happy, and by the look of him so was Harry. While he was engaged in a rapid-fire exchange with Eddy Napier and James Colville, Nadine Bancroft detached herself from

Matt and Jassy and a group of Wilding relations and drew her new daughter-in-law aside. Nadine was a very elegant woman in her fifties, with expertly cut greying hair that had once been as dark as Frances's own. Harry and Charlotte had inherited their looks from their father, and this small, slim woman was the exact opposite of everything Frances had pictured beforehand.

'Harry says you know everything about the terms of the will, my dear,' she said. 'I can't tell you how pleased and happy I am that he's found a girl willing to marry him with all faults, so to speak.'

'Faults?' Frances smiled serenely and shook her head. 'It's not Harry's fault his inheritance was left with such stringent conditions, and he works so terribly hard to keep this place going that I'm only too happy to try and help.'

'Even to the point of trying to produce a son as soon as possible?' There was sympathy mingled with humour in Nadine's magnificent dark grey eyes. 'You're very young.'

'I'm twenty-two, Mrs Bancroft—not all that young, and I love children.' Frances gave a little shrug. 'And if I don't achieve the desired son I'll be very sorry for Harry, but not for myself. My family's not wealthy, so I won't miss what I've never had. But I know Harry hates to see the house suffering any neglect.'

'His father was a very unrelenting man in some ways, and never gave me an inkling of the wretched proviso he added to the will.' Nadine's eyes hardened fleetingly. 'If I *had* known I'd have done my utmost to dissuade him. Even my small annuity had strings, you know—no remarriage. But I gladly gave that up to marry Dexter, who, as you can see, is a warm, loving man, even if he's not all that plump in the pocket.' She gestured towards the big, tanned man chatting so easily to Frances's relatives. He looked genial and good-tempered and plainly worshipped the ground on which his wife walked. 'I only hope Harry is as good a husband to you as Dexter is to me.' She leaned forward suddenly and kissed her new daughter-in-law's cheek, then smiled and changed the subject by asking for details of the honeymoon.

A honeymoon was not on the agenda, in actual fact, Frances confided. The wedding had been arranged for one of the three days a week when Curthoys Court was closed to the public, and apart from taking the other two off from his job, Harry had asked Frances if she minded postponing a real honeymoon until later in the year when the property market quietened down. Frances had assured him she had no objection at all; she had reached a very interesting stage with the archives and would be quite pleased to get on with them. Harry's face had been a study. His idea had been to spend a couple of quiet days together just getting used to being married, he had informed her, not to drive her back up to the attic the moment his ring was on her finger.

Frances laughed as she told Nadine about his indignation and Harry turned back to her at once, sliding an arm round her waist.

'Well, Mother?' he demanded. 'What do you think of the new chatelaine of Curthoys Court?'

'That,' said Nadine with mock severity, 'is not a tactful question, my son. It's traditional for us to dislike each other on sight, is it not, Frances?'

'I hope not!' Frances smiled with beguiling confidence. 'As far as I'm concerned I think I'm very fortunate in my choice of mother-in-law.'

Soon afterwards the Napiers, including Eddy, came to say their goodbyes. Caroline gave Frances a quick hug, then stood back, her face wreathed in smiles.

'We've left Sam with Charles's mother, so we must get back before the poor old darling expires with exhaustion.' She gave a wave around her at the ancient, impressive hall thronged with people. 'It's all so wonderful, Frances, like a fairy-tale.'

'With me in the role of fairy godmother,' put in Eddy Napier, his eyes gleaming at Frances in a way that made her hackles rise. 'Give credit where it's due! If it hadn't been for me you two would never have met.' He was shorter and more heavily built than Harry, and despite the conventional morning suit worn for his function as best man, still managed to look raffish and overpowering with his shock of red hair and the beard that was longer since Frances had last seen him. She gave him a wry, cool little smile.

'Not a role I'd have cast you in myself,' she murmured, 'but thank you for recommending me to Harry in the first place.'

'My pleasure.' Eddy bent his red head and kissed the hand she surrendered to him unwillingly. 'Not that I had the least idea how it would turn out. I was under the impression you intended marrying some childhood sweetheart.'

'But she changed her mind,' cut in Harry swiftly. 'As you can see, she married me instead,'

'And very glad I am that you did,' he told Frances later that evening, when the last of the guests had finally departed, and the bridal pair were eating the belated, special supper Mrs Bates had prepared with such loving care. Afterwards they sat in the morning-room over coffee, chatting just as they had done on so many evenings. Only this was no ordinary evening, as Frances was disturbingly aware, however much she tried to pretend it was. For one thing they were dressed differently, not in the silk organza and grey formality of their wedding clothes, it was true, but she was in one of her new dresses, and Harry was wearing a suit, and, the biggest difference of all, they had dressed at the same time in the rooms they would share from now on as man and wife.

For Harry the change was minimal. He would merely be sharing the room he had slept in since he inherited. Originally used for guests, since it had its own dressing-room and bathroom, the small suite had the advantage of a self-contained situation in a small wing that could be completely cut off during public days. Frances had tried her best not to feel ill at ease when Harry ushered her into his big bedroom, with its view of the moat and spinney, but since he immediately retired to the dressing-room to change his clothes, and conducted a matter-of-fact conversation through the half-open door while he did so, the fleeting moment of awkwardness was smoothed over painlessly as Frances substituted moss-green silk for the ivory organza. She gave Harry a smile of gratitude when he strolled back into the room, knotting his tie and telling her to get a move on as though this were the habit of years instead of their first night together.

'Nice welcoming smile, Mrs Curthoys,' he commented, eyes gleaming. 'Stunning dress, too.'

'Thank you, Harry. For being so understanding, I mean. You may have to make allowances for me at first. But I'll get used to—to everything as quickly as possible.' Frances touched her hand to Harry's cheek, and he turned his head to kiss her palm.

'Of course you will,' he assured her. 'And remember, the only real difference now is that you'll be sleeping here instead of at the gatehouse.'

It might be the only difference, but to Frances it was one that loomed very large in her mind at that moment, taking precedence over everything else to such an extent she hardly knew what she ate during supper. It was a relief when it was over and they were settled by the fire Bates had insisted was necessary. Frances sighed as she relaxed in her chair.

'I'm more glad than I can say that you did marry me instead of your accountant,' repeated Harry.

She turned her head against the chairback and smiled at him. 'It's a bit early for statements like that.'

'Not in the least.' Harry took off his jacket and subsided again into his chair. 'I don't foresee any change of opinion. Not every girl would want to hear me rabbiting on about roof repairs and whether the central heating system is likely to pack in——'

'Heavens, is it, Harry?' she asked, startled, and he chuckled.

'You see? Instant gratifying interest!'

'Prompted by the fact that I feel the cold!'

Harry grinned lazily. 'I guarantee personally to do all I can to prevent hypothermia becoming a problem for you.'

Frances went bright red, and looked away, and Harry jumped to his feet.

'Spot of brandy,' he said briskly. 'That's what you need.'

She giggled. 'Dr Curthoys's remedy for all ills!'

He laughed and handed her a glass. 'Up you get,' he commanded.

Frances did so, grumbling. 'I was very comfortable there, Harry.'

He sat down in her place and pulled her down on his lap. 'I think we'll both be happier like this. I will, certainly, for obvious reasons, and perhaps if we snuggle up together and chat about our day, or whatever else comes into our heads, you may relax and forget the jitters which are very obviously bugging you. Am I right?'

Frances relaxed against him, comforted at once by the physical contact, since there was nothing in the least importunate in the way Harry held her close, and she forgot her nerves in her appreciation of Harry's comments on some of the confections worn by the feminine guests.

'All those hats,' she said idly. 'I was very impressed by the one Mrs Bates was wearing.'

'Fearsome thing, wasn't it! Dolly's up in the clouds, you know, Frances. I think she had you earmarked for your future role the minute she laid eyes on you in the office, even if you did look like a drowned rat.'

'Rat!'

'Kitten, then.' He hugged her closer. 'You probably appealed to her maternal instincts.'

'Hm.' Frances twisted round to look up at him speculatively. 'Were you sorry for me too? Is that why you gave me the job?'

'Sorry for you! The kitten impression wasn't so far out, in fact. You spat and showed your claws pretty sharpish when I said I'd had a man in mind for the job.' He looked down his prominent Curthoys nose at her. 'You all but suggested I was gay.'

'You might have been, for all I knew.'

'Thanks a lot. Have you changed your mind since?'

'Yes.' Frances sipped at her brandy. 'After all, those old newspaper stories about you when you were young can't all have been wrong. There was a girl draped round you in practically every photograph.'

Harry shifted her a little so that he could reach for his own glass. 'There weren't that many, I didn't spend my entire college career drinking and womanising, I'll have you know. I emerged with a degree in geography. Not as exalted as your history degree, but respectable enough to astound my family. Unfortunately my father died beforehand, or he might have relented over the money.'

'In which case you would now be married to your Annabel, and I would never have met you,' finished Frances solemnly.

Harry said nothing for a moment or two, then his hand turned her face up to his. 'Very likely,' he agreed softly, which was a far from satisfactory response from Frances's point of view. 'Nevertheless,' he went on casually, 'Annabel is married to her moneybags, your old chum is shackled to his Scottish lady-love and we—why we just have each other, and we shall just have to make the best of things, shan't we?'

Frances never made the protest that rose to her lips since Harry stifled it by kissing her with a finality that indicated very plainly he intended to start making the best of things at that very moment, and since she was well aware that her co-operation in this particular area was the main reason why she was now Harry's wife, Frances let him, with a passivity that brought Harry to a halt almost immediately. He raised his head to look down at her eyes.

'Please, Frances, don't just *let* me make love to you. I want the response you gave me that first time, on New Year's Eve.' He ran a fingertip delicately down her cheek. 'Don't just lie there as though I'm exacting payment for this.' He touched the heavy gold band on her finger.

Frances felt guilty. 'I didn't mean to, Harry, but I said

you'd need to make allowances for me. I'm not really all that good at this sort of thing.'

He frowned and held her closer. 'What sort of thing?'

Frances flushed painfully and tried to turn her head away, but Harry kept his hand firmly beneath her chin so he could see her face.

'Well—Chris used to get impatient because I wasn't keen on the sex thing. I liked the kissing and the touching and so on, but when it came to the rest of it I was a great disappointment, I know, which is probably why he didn't want me in the end.'

Harry swore under his breath and reached out an arm for the decanter. 'Here, have some more brandy.' He made her swallow quite a hefty mouthful before allowing her to curl back against him. Frances felt better at once as the warmth of the spirit spread through her, liking the steady beat of Harry's heart beneath her cheek, and the clean, familiar scent of his skin, and she wriggled a little, sliding her arm around him as she burrowed closer. 'That's more like it,' he said rather breathlessly. 'Now what's all this nonsense about being no good, for God's sake? Absolute rot. You weren't in the least disappointing the last time I had you on my lap like this—and don't say *you* didn't like it because I'm a bit more experienced in this particular field than you and I know damn well you did.'

Frances nodded. 'I did. I admit it. But you and I never got beyond the kissing stage. You'd probably have been just as disappointed as Chris if we had.'

'Then there's only one thing to do. Let's go to bed and find out.' Harry pushed her to her feet and kept her firmly in the crook of his arm as he put out the lights and led her through the house to the stairs where he paused, a rather wicked smile on his face. 'I know I should pick you up and carry you in the best tradition of all fictional heroes, but I warn you now that if I sprint up there with you in my arms and carry you all the way to our room, there'll be no question of anything more than a kiss and a cuddle, my darling bride, because that's all I'll be fit for!'

Frances laughed as Harry took her hand and pulled her up the staircase. Suddenly his words seemed exquisitely funny and she began to laugh helplessly, unable to stop. Harry eyed her in alarm as he opened the door of their bedroom.

'My God, you're not going to have hysterics now, are you?'

'No,' she gasped, and leaned against him weakly. 'I'm all right, really.'

'Good.' He bent to scoop her up and carried her across the room to deposit her in the middle of the bed. 'That much, dear heart, is well within my capabilities,' he informed her with a grin, then lowered himself beside her and began to kiss her, gently at first, then with a growing heat and intensity that put an end to her laughter very effectively. His hands, which had been roving over the thin silk of her dress, slid beneath it to find the curve of her breasts, his fingers teasing streaks of fire from her nipples that made her open her mouth to him with a sudden gasp of agonised pleasure and instantly his tongue slid within to probe the soft secret places and entwine with hers. Frances felt his body tense and his hands shake as he slid the dress from her shoulders and smoothed it away until she lay in the brief ivory satin underwear bought to wear beneath her wedding dress. Harry slid away and propped himself up to look at her, smiling down at her flushed face and bright, uncertain eyes.

'What is it?' he asked softly.

'Should I still be wearing my shoes?'

Harry threw back his head and laughed delightedly, then ran his fingers delicately up her thigh. 'Why not? Very erotic, combined with stockings and suspenders.'

'So I've heard.' Frances smiled with growing confidence, aware that her inhibitions appeared to have drowned in her last mouthful of brandy. She stretched deliberately, and Harry's eyes narrowed. He began to take off the rest of her clothes with fingers that shook and grew clumsy in his haste, and she helped him, deeply gratified when dark, unfamiliar colour rose a long Harry's cheekbones. The shy invitation in her eyes made him swallow hard as he stripped himself of his own clothes with flattering speed and flung himself down again beside her to hold her close.

'Are you cold?' he asked, as he felt her tremble against him.

'A little—but you said you knew a remedy for that,' she reminded him huskily.

Harry chuckled breathlessly and embarked on a series of delicate, nibbling kisses all over her face. 'I thought you said you weren't very good at all this, Frances.'

'I must be honest and say that with you I seem to like it much more than—than previously,' she admitted, where-upon Harry fell to kissing her so fiercely that it was some time before she continued. 'It's from now on that the problems usually arise, Harry.'

'I think they won't,' he said positively. 'In fact, I'll bet you anything you like there'll be no problems at all. If I'm wrong you get the pearls I was keeping to hand over on our first anniversary. Agreed?'

Frances gave a smothered little laugh and surrendered her mouth to his. To her surprise and delight what followed bore as little resemblance to her limited experience of lovemaking as vintage champagne does to lemonade as her entire body caught fire in response to the loving skill of Harry's seeking mouth and hands. Her own hands grew urgent with the need to explore and caress, and she felt a fierce joy as Harry's muscles tensed beneath her tentative fingers and he gave a sharp gasp of almost unbearable pleasure as their bodies finally merged in a union impossible to resist an instant longer. Skill, or lack of it, was forgotten as she became submerged, overturned in the flood of sensation that swept her headlong to the blissful culmination she had secretly believed happened only in fiction. Frances clung to Harry convulsively as the storm broke, and he held her fast as the shock-waves receded and at last she lay still, her face buried against his throat as their breathing quietened and their heartbeats slowed.

After a long, long interval, Harry stirred a little. 'Sorry,' he muttered, 'I'm afraid you don't get the pearls.'

Frances stretched a little, still dazed and wondering, and parted her lips against his throat as she laughed softly. 'I thought not. So what shall I give *you* instead?'

'Let me see now . . .' He paused, pretending to consider, then ran the tip of his tongue round the delicate, sensitive whorls of her ear. Frances shivered, her fingers digging involuntarily into his back. 'Just—this.' Harry moved against her, and she gave a stifled little moan.

'Now?'

'Now!'

It was much later when, only-half-surfacing from sleep in the darkness, Frances woke disorientated, dimly conscious of an arm heavy across her waist.

'Chris?' she mumbled indistinctly, still half-asleep, then the arm holding her withdrew with a sudden violence that brought her back sharply to full recall of where she was. And who was beside her. The light snapped on and Frances stared, stricken, into the frosted fury in Harry's eyes, their hostility giving his face the look of a stranger.

'Bad manners, darling,' he drawled, and ice dripped from every word. 'Not polite to mutter other men's names on your wedding night, Mrs Curthoys, ma'am. Particularly that one. You made me a promise, too, that you would not—remember? I have a strong objection to sharing my nuptial couch with a former lover, unreasonable though it may seem.'

Frances tried to move away but he held her by the chin and jerked her face up to his, and her eyes widened in swift resentment, their flecks flashing fire in the lamplight.

'I'm not *your* first choice, either,' she reminded him proudly.

'But I wasn't burbling about Annabel in *my* sleep, little cat. I knew damn well who *I* was making love to . . .' Abruptly the ice in Harry's eyes changed and they grew molten with a look that made Frances tremble. 'Perhaps I'd better help you clear up any last lingering confusion regarding bedfellows,' he muttered thickly, and his mouth came crushing down on hers as he pinned her beneath him.

Frances resisted fiercely for a moment or two, but it was useless. Harry was surprisingly strong, and what's more he was in a towering rage, and she gave up the fruitless contest after a while and freed her mouth to whisper drily, 'Turn off the light. *Please!*'

His soft laugh raised the hairs along her spine. 'Oh, no, Frances. No mistakes this time. Open those cat's eyes of yours and look at me. *Look* at me! That's better. I want you to see very clearly just *who* is making love to you. This is your lawfully wedded husband. Harry. So remember in future—or I'll be obliged to keep jogging your memory, won't I? Now—who am I?'

Frances clenched her teeth and moved her head away, refusing to answer, and he slid away from her. For a moment she thought he had relented, then she felt her knees pulled apart and let out a hoarse, incredulous cry at the weight of his head between her thighs and the flame that shot through her entire body as she felt his tongue in a caress she had never experienced before.

'Oh, please—stop!' she gasped. 'You mustn't—you can't——'

Harry raised his head and shook back his hair to look at her in triumph as he saw the shock on her face. 'Oh, but I must—and I can,' and he resumed his caresses to such effect that, utterly humiliated by her own lack of self-control, Frances burned in the throes of a climax she was helpless to prevent.

Almost at once Harry slid up the bed and dragged her into his arms, breathing raggedly as he forced her face up to his with ungentle fingers. 'Open your eyes,' he commanded. 'Open them now, Frances, and look at me.'

With a frantic sob she obeyed, sinking her teeth into her bottom lip.

'Well, well,' he said derisively. 'I rather fancy I hit on

something new to you then, didn't I?' He shook her slightly. 'Didn't I?'

She nodded disdainfully and turned her head away. 'Can I go to sleep now, please?'

'Oh, no, not yet,' he drawled. 'You, er, enjoyed yourself all on your own then, kitten. Now it's my turn.' And he began to make love to her all over again, and to Frances's shame and outrage brought her to fulfilment once more before giving himself up to the convulsive pleasure of his own release.

CHAPTER TEN

'LETTER here from Eddy Napier,' remarked Harry over breakfast a month or so later.

The day was warm, early though it was, but it was not summer heat which made Frances so disinclined to linger in bed in the mornings. On that very first morning she had been up and dressed long before Harry, establishing a routine she had kept to rigidly ever since. It seemed utterly pointless to lie there in bed when she woke at dawn every day, often long before. Frances detested that first moment when her mind woke fully to the prospect of another day of keeping up appearances in front of other people. Even Mrs Bates never seemed to suspect that things were not quite as they should be for the newly weds, because Harry was so skilful in adopting a loving, affectionate manner towards his bride when anyone else was present. He dropped it quickly enough the moment they were alone, however, she thought bitterly. There had been no nonsense about separate bedrooms, either. That was something else Harry had made crystal clear right from the start, and since Frances was only too conscious of her obligations in this area she never offered any argument on the subject, nor ever refused to let him make love to her, which was more often than she had dreamed possible before her marriage.

Frances was determined to keep to her agreement to try to provide Harry with the son whose appearance in the world would release his father's inheritance and, hopefully, at the same time release his mother from the bitter-sweet anguish of her conjugal duties. These days she could feel sympathy for the dead Arabella. She had been troubled by her husband's attentions too—though not in remotely the same way as the present Curthoys bride.

To Frances her wedding night had been a watershed. In

a mere matter of hours her life had abandoned its former course and taken off in a new, uncharted direction, and it was one of life's bitter little ironies that the very night which had ousted Chris from her heart for all time also resulted in estrangement from her husband before their new relationship was even hours old. At some time during those first ecstatic moments in Harry's arms Frances had been overwhelmed by the discovery that she loved her new husband utterly. She had liked him from the start, enjoyed his company, grown to respect him considerably, but on that never to be forgotten night his tender, consummate skill brought to life a physical passion she had never even dreamed she was capable of feeling, and with it came the realisation that she loved Harry in every way possible. She realised now that her feelings for Chris had been those of a girl for a boy. Harry Curthoys, for all his casual, understated charm, was adult; a man in every sense of the word, and she loved him as a woman loves a man, and would do for the rest of her life.

It was a thought which brought little joy. Another reason for her weariness was the constant battle she fought to keep him in ignorance of her new-found feelings towards him. Sometimes, during the night, when he wrung every last response of which she was capable from her gasping, writhing body, she drew blood from her bottom lip as she bit it hard to keep back the words of love that yearned for expression as she stifled her moans of pleasure in his arms. Theirs was a fiery, wordless coming together, with none of the delicacy of that first idyllic experience. Tenderness had been supplanted by savagery as Harry took the revenge he seemed to crave night after night for that one first unconscious slip of the tongue that transformed a loving friend into an implacable, demanding lover by night and a polite, casual stranger by day. Frances's mouth turned down in a bitter little smile as she stared at the letter she was holding. Life with Harry Curthoys was like being married to Dr Jekyll and Mr Hyde. She looked up and coloured a little to find Harry regarding her quizzically.

'Amusing letter?' he enquired.

'Just Jassy going on at length about the perfection of Thomas Matthew Wilding. Quite the most wonderful baby ever born, according to his mother.' Frances put the letter down quickly, the subject of babies hardly one she cared to discuss at the present time. 'I'm sorry—you said something about a letter, too.'

'From Eddy Napier,' repeated Harry patiently. 'He'd like to come and stay. Says he appreciates accomodation in the house is difficult when it's open to the public, but is perfectly happy to put up at the gatehouse. Any objection?'

Frances shrugged indifferently. 'No, of course not. Ask Dolly how she feels about it.'

'I'd rather know how *you* feel about it.' Harry held out his cup for more coffee and Frances filled it, thinking how tired he looked. There were dark marks beneath the eyes that rarely seemed to smile any more. The exhausting nights and work-filled days were making a mark on both of them, as she knew only too well from her own mirror.

'He's not my most favourite person, I admit, but he's one of your oldest friends,' she said coolly, 'so ask him along by all means.'

Harry looked at her curiously. 'Why don't you like him, Frances?'

'No particular reason.'

'There must be something!'

Frances returned his look levelly. 'It's not worth talking about really, but if you must know I suppose it's because I'm not overfond of men who regard anything young and female as fair game.'

Harry's eyebrows rose, and the corners of his mouth twitched. 'You mean Eddy made a pass at you?'

'Several. He seemed to be under the mistaken impression that I was at the Napiers' to entertain the famous visiting artist rather than look after Sam.' Frances's eyes kindled at the memory.

'What exactly do you mean by pass?'

Frances eyed her amused husband disdainfully. 'All very

entertaining to you no doubt, but to me, as an employee of the Napiers, it was extremely awkward. Men like him should know better than to mess about with the servants.'

'Oh, come now, Frances! I don't suppose for a moment Eddy ever thought of you as a servant—just as an attractive girl. And from time immemorial Eddy Napier's first instinct when near a pretty girl is to grab. What did he do?' he added curiously.

Frances looked away uncomfortably. 'At first it was just a squeeze of the waist whenever I couldn't avoid passing him on the landing. Then one day the ghastly female— Sorcha something—he'd brought with him persuaded Caroline Napier to take her shopping. Sam was having a nap and Eddy Napier ran me to earth in the utility-room at Glebe House and shut the door, knowing we were virtually alone in the house.'

Harry's face darkened. 'And then?'

'I happened to be ironing. I put the iron down on his hand. His left hand as it happened, but I wasn't discriminating. It could just as easily have been the one that wields the brush.'

Harry whistled. 'My God! Eddy never told me that.'

'Hardly surprising.' Frances gave a mirthless laugh. 'He howled like a banshee, woke Sam, who began to roar, so I had to quieten Sam down, slap a burn dressing on Eddy's left hand and a Scotch in his right, and by the time the others came home the three of us were playing with Sam's train set in apparent amity. Eddy and his lady went off to France suddenly next day, and after that I never saw him again until the wedding.'

Harry scratched his chin, looking at her warily. 'Eddy wants to paint your portrait.'

Frances stared at him incredulously. 'You're not serious!'

'He intends it as the wedding present he's never given us.'

'But you can't want a portrait of *me*, Harry!'

'Why not?' he said carelessly. 'There usually is a portrait of the Curthoys brides.'

'I haven't seen one of your mother.'

'I gave it to Dexter for a wedding present.'

'Oh.' Frances sighed wearily. 'But it's different as far as I'm concerned. I mean, our marriage is just an arrangement——'

'Which probably makes it no different from all other Curthoys marriages,' he said caustically. 'I don't suppose many of your predecessors married for love, either, unless one counts my mother, and I don't think her initial feelings for my father survived very long.' He jumped up restlessly from the table. 'Whereas yours for me never even got off the ground at all, did they?'

'That's not fair——'

'Fair! All's fair in love and war, so they say. I didn't think it particularly *fair* when my loving bride murmured someone else's name in my ear on our wedding night either, but that's how the cookie crumbles, dear heart. For better for worse, I think we both said, and now we're stuck with it!'

'You can always divorce me,' said Frances, tight-lipped.

Harry smiled at her tauntingly. 'On what grounds? God knows, you don't refuse me my conjugal rights, or whatever the term is. And I believe infidelity needs to be a little more physical than the mental variety you indulge in.'

'I don't indulge in infidelity of any kind! How many times do I have to keep saying the same thing? Once and once only I said Chris's name——'

'In my arms, in my bed, and during the course of our wedding night,' he broke in bitterly.

'I was half-asleep and hardly knew where I was,' said Frances in despair. 'I've told you before, I must have assumed you were Chris because he's the one I've known all my life.'

'And the man you were accustomed to sleeping with, of course.'

Frances lifted her chin haughtily. 'What I did before I met you is not really any of your concern, but since you've insisted on turning one microscopic molehill into something resembling Mount Everest, you may as well know that I never have actually slept with Chris at all.'

Harry's eyes narrowed. 'I dont believe you,' he said flatly.

'As you please.' She began piling the breakfast things rapidly on a tray. 'Nevertheless I might point out that one of the disadvantages of living next door to each other is that one's never really able to—cohabit on one's home ground. It would have embarrassed my father, and heaven knows how Mrs Bradley would have reacted. Then at our respective universities I shared a flat with four other girls, and Chris shared with three men, literally no room at the inn.' She smiled scathingly. 'It was only very recently that we finally got to that stage, anyway—I was a remarkably late developer in matters of the flesh.'

'So where did your amorous confrontations take place— back of a car? The drawing-room sofa when your parents were out?' The distaste in Harry's voice whipped colour into Frances's cheeks.

'The goings-on of the lower orders must no doubt be of tremendous interest to people like you, Harry Curthoys,' she said, stung, 'but I don't intend to satisfy mere prurient curiosity, just the same. I admit we made one or two highly unsatisfactory amatory attempts, and because he's the only other man who ever even came near to making love to me I suppose that was the reason I said Chris's name that night.' Her voice shook and she snatched up the tray, making the cups wobble dangerously.

'Here—let me.' Harry tried to take the tray from her but she resisted fiercely, glaring at him from hostile, wet eyes.

'I might remind you that I don't keep harping about your precious Annabel, and don't tell me you didn't share a bed with her often enough, and probably dozens of other women besides!'

'Are you jealous?' he asked swiftly, and a gleam lit his eyes for an instant.

Frances swept past him, her eyes derisive. 'Why on earth should I be jealous, Harry?' She went off to the kitchen, able to hear Harry's voluble curses quite clearly as he strode off to the stables to get out the car. Frances winced as she heard him gunning the engine of the Range Rover away down the drive, and washed up at top speed so she could take refuge in the attic, away from the keen eyes of Mrs Bates.

She dashed angry tears from her eyes as she climbed dispiritedly up the stairs to an attic a great deal less chaotic now than it had been when she started. Mason, the gardener, had put up some shelves for her, and ledgers and files were arranged now in orderly rows. A great many documents were already stored in acid-free ventilated boxes in the regulated temperature of the new muniment room, which was better suited to them than the extremes of the attic. In the beginning Frances's task had seemed Herculean to her on some days, but now, after working doggedly for the entire time since the wedding, she felt she could see light at the end of the tunnel.

Today, however, it was almost impossible to concentrate on the inventory she was typing. The scene at the breakfast table had upset Frances badly. Not that it was the first, by any means—ever since their wedding night Harry seemed unable to leave the subject alone. She gave up even trying to work after a while and put her head down on her arms and indulged in a few tears, as she thought of the other problem troubling her, in addition to Harry's hostility. Lately she was troubled by vivid dreams of Hal and Arabella, who seemed inextricably confused with Harry and herself in their unhappiness, and several times in the past month had woken up, shivering and terrified in the middle of the night, to find herself in some other part of the house, most often in the muniment room, that one-time resting place for the coffins of the dead.

Frances sat up straight, making a resolution to forget Arabella and Hal Curthoys, consign them to the past where they belonged, and concentrate her energies on putting the present to rights instead. Perhaps then the sleep-walking would stop. The door opened a little later to admit Bates, who came into the hot, airless attic carrying a tray with an

insulated jug and a plate of Mrs Bates's freshly baked
walnut biscuits.

'Good morning, Miss Frances. My wife thought you
might prefer a cold drink to coffee, since it's so hot today.
She's made you some fresh lemonade.'

'Lovely,' sighed Frances. 'Tell her I shan't want too
much for lunch, though—it's too warm.'

Bates looked non-committal. 'I believe she mentioned
something about a seafood salad, Miss Frances. And Mr
Harry rang with a message for you. It seems he forgot to
remind you at breakfast that he's dining with his uncle Mr
Dangerfield in Oxford this evening and is likely to be late.'

Frances found she was rather relieved that Harry would
be out for the evening, and when she had finished her stint
in the attic took a long, leisurely bath with a novel, not even
bothering to dress afterwards. Cool and comfortable in a
thin white lawn nightdress and dressing-gown, she curled
up in her usual chair in the morning-room later on to watch
a programme about a Saxon burial ground while she
nibbled at a cheese sandwich and drank more lemonade.
When there was no sign of Harry by ten she took a stroll in
the twilight before going to bed. It was still quite warm and
she went as she was, not bothering to put on a coat since her
only company was the quarter-moon which hung in the
violet sky. It seemed to mock her solitary state, and Frances
gave it a withering look as she wandered aimlessly past
Mason's lovingly tended flowerbeds and bent to count the
stars reflected in the still waters of the moat.

The air was heavy with the scent of newly cut grass and
made her oddly restless, reluctant to return to the house,
and she ventured further, away from the gardens and on
into the park, deliberately following the path to the church.
As it came into view Frances halted, frowning a she peered
along the line of yews leading to the door, which was open.
A light burned inside and she hesitated, wondering if Bates
had forgotten to lock it. It seemed best to find out, and she
went down the path on silent, slippered feet and went
inside.

'Bates? Are you there?' For some reason her query came out in a mere whisper, she found, and smiled wryly. There was something about the atmosphere of a church, however small, that discouraged a raised voice. There was no reply and Frances turned to leave, then hesitated again and shrugged as she went down the aisle. She could never resist a visit to Hal Curthoys however often she came into the church and she wandered into the side chapel, patting the battered stone effigies of his ancestors as she passed on her way to the railing separating his memorial from theirs. As always, her fingers closed round the slim iron bars as she gazed through them at the figure of the sleeping man, and she leaned there in dreamy reverie, thinking sadly of the gallant Royalist who had fought for his king so bravely only to suffer death at the hands of his own wife.

'I feel for you, Hal,' she murmured. 'You deserved a better fate than the one Arabella had in store for you.'

Frances shook her head impatiently, and laughed a little at her own absurdity, then stooped to reach through the railings for the faded flowers in the vase placed near Hal's marble-booted feet. At which moment the church was plunged into darkness and Frances's breathless cry of dismay was drowned by the clang of the door as it closed.

Blind panic overtook her immediately and she turned to run, calling for Bates, only to fall headlong over one of the stone tombs. She lay winded and gasping for a moment, overcome by sheer claustrophobic fear in the deathly quiet darkness. After a moment or two she pulled herself together, telling herself not to be such a ninny as she tried to get up, but a red-hot needle of pain shot through her ankle and she gritted her teeth as she manoeuvered herself into a sitting position, cursing herself for coming into the church in the first place.

For a while Frances fumed in frustration, then became aware that she was no longer warm at all. She shivered a little as her eyes strained to see, gradually becoming accustomed to the gloom in the starlight filtering through the windows. With determination she looked about her to orientate herself before making a move. She was propped up against the crumbling stone feet of one Nicholas Curthoys she thought, by her position, from which she could just make out the faint glimmer of the cloth on the altar. To her left she could see, with unnerving clarity, the gleaming whiteness of Hal's slumbering figure, illumined by the moon shining in through the window directly above it.

Frances looked away hurriedly, finding that the reclining figure looked far too lifelike for her peace of mind under the present circumstances, and with an apology to their owner she grabbed Nicholas's stone feet and managed to haul herself upright. Gingerly she put her weight on the wrenched ankle, and drew in a deep breath of relief. It was sore—in fact it hurt abominably—but it was definitely only a wrench and she could hobble on it after a fashion as long as she fought down the urge to run. Feeling like an uncoordinated crab, she scuttled as fast as she could to the back of the church, grabbing the end of a pew here and there along the way. When she reached the wall with the light switches she scrabbled frantically over it until she found them and with a sob of relief turned them on.

The mere prescence of light was enough to bring Frances back to near normality, and to restore the church, which had been disturbingly eerie in the darkness, to its normal charm. The door, as expected, was locked, and after rattling the handle and banging on the timbers for a while, Frances was forced to resign herself to as patient a wait as possible until she was discovered. She felt sure Harry would see the lights in the church when he came home and realise where she was. In the mean time Frances decided that the sensible thing to do was to get her weight off her sore foot. She gathered up a couple of hassocks from the floor, arranged them as a pillow on the nearest pew to the door and lay down carefully, disposing the long skirt of her dressing-gown over her legs to keep as warm as possible before she closed her eyes and tried to relax. This was easier said than done. For one thing she was cold, and for another she was very uncomfortable on the hard, slippery wood of her makeshift couch, and, however hard she tried not to think about it, Frances heartily disliked the experience of being locked alone in the church at night with only the tombs of Hal Curthoys and his ancestors for company. She would have given anything to hear Harry's voice. She longed for his physical presence with an intensity that came near to vanquishing her cold and fear, and hugged her arms across her chest fiercely, vowing to be so sweet and wonderful and loving to him in future he would have no alternative but to respond in kind. She wanted the old, charming Harry back, the man she had married, instead of the forbidding stranger who had taken his place since their wedding night.

Time crawled by. Frances tried to hurry it up by reciting in her head all the poetry she had learned at school, the lyrics of all the songs she knew, until at last, in spite of the dull throb in her ankle and the sheer discomfort of her resting place, she dozed uneasily, troubled almost immediately by fragments of dreams that flashed through her subconscious like colours in a kaleidoscope. There was Harry, with smiling eyes that turned cold and changed to the dark, guilt-filled gaze of Arabella.

Frances stirred restlessly, half-waking, then slid back into sleep again as Hal's face swam into focus. Wearing the proud self-confidence of the youth in the miniature for a fleeting moment before it altered, aged and grew lined with disillusion. His eyes, grey like Harry's, drew her like magnets and his hand beckoned her to follow him. Filled with dread she tried to resist, but in fascinated obedience stumbled after the glimmering figure which led her to the side chapel and drifted through the railing with a sigh she felt rather than heard, as Hal lay down and buried his face in the crook of his arm. His other hand lifted and beckoned, and then there were voices and noise and shock and Harry was shaking her and prising her fingers loose from their manacle-like grip of the railings fencing in Hal's tomb.

'What the hell do you think you're doing?' snarled

Harry. His eyes blazed in his ashen face as he shook her mercilessly, and Frances blinked and gasped and cried out at the pain in her ankle.

'Oh, please—stop it, Harry!' she implored, and glared up into his incensed face, her face flushing as she caught sight of Bates, anxious and distressed behind Harry's shoulder.

'Are you all right, Miss Frances?' he asked, distraught. 'I must have locked you in when I finished my rounds about ten——'

'Ten!' Harry shot back his shirt-cuff to look at his watch. 'It's gone midnight now.' His anger began to subside as he saw Frances shiver, and he took off his jacket and wrapped it round her. 'God, you must be chilled right through to the bone after a couple of hours in this place, even on a warm night like this. What the devil possessed you to come here at this time of night?'

'I wanted some fresh air,' she said woodenly, 'so I went for a stroll before going to bed. It was so warm, I didn't bother with a coat, and I caught sight of a light here, so I came to investigate.'

'And I never realised you were inside,' said Bates in distress. 'I went to throw the dead flowers away, you see, and I just came back and put out the lights and closed the door as usual. I had already checked up inside the church earlier, and assumed it was empty.'

'Which it should have been,' said Harry grimly, then forced a smile for Bates, who looked the picture of guilt. 'Don't blame yourself, Bates, please. It wasn't your fault. Blame my wife's fascination for the place.'

'Yes, indeed,' added Frances emphatically. 'It was a very stupid thing to do, and I'm very sorry to have worried you.'

'You cut along, Bates. Tell Dolly all's well, and you can both get a good night's sleep,' said Harry kindly, and with a few last reassurances as to Frances's well-being Bates hurried of.

'Well,' said Harry, and leaned against the railing Frances was still clutching for support. The anger faded from his eyes as they rested on her apprehensive face. 'I really thought you'd run off and left me when I found you were missing, you know.'

She frowned. '*Left* you? Why?'

'The house was empty, the bed hadn't been slept in—what else was I to think?' Harry's eyes glinted. 'I even looked up in your damned attic before I finally knocked at the gatehouse to see if Dolly knew where you were, which nearly gave her a heart attack. I took it you'd seized the opportunity of my absence tonight to take off.'

'Without any clothes?' Frances asked drily.

He gave a short laugh. 'I was in too much of a panic to check on your wardrobe. Somehow I got it into my thick head you'd gone home to your father.'

'Don't tell me you rang him, Harry!'

'No. Even I, idiot though I am, stopped short of giving him a shock like that at this time of night.'

'Thank God for that,' she said fervently, then bit her lip as she inadvertently put her weight on the injured ankle.

'What is it?' he asked swiftly. 'Are you hurt?'

'Bates didn't see me when he came back to lock the church because I was round here——'

'With Hal, as usual!'

'Exactly. And in the darkness I tripped and sprawled on the floor, giving my ankle a bit of a wrench at the same time.' The smile she gave him wavered uncertainly and Harry cursed and knelt in front of her on the cold stone of the floor.

'Which one?' he said tersely, and she raised the offending foot in its flimsy white mule. Harry took it in his hand gently and probed the bones delicately. 'No break, obviously, but a slight sprain, I think—it's a bit swollen. Not very sensible shoes for walking, are they?'

'I never intended to go so far.'

Harry jumped to his feet and looked at her searchingly. 'I didn't pursue the matter in front of Bates but now perhaps you'll explain why I had to wake you when I found you here hanging like grim death to these railings.'

'I must have been walking in my sleep again,' she said

reluctantly, refusing to meet his eyes. 'I stretched out on a pew at the back of the church, intending to stay there until I was found, but I had a dream. I dreamt that Hal Curthoys was beckoning me to join him—in there.' Frances gestured towards the tomb with a shudder. 'Needless to say I didn't fancy the idea, and must have been clinging to the railings to avoid doing what he wanted.'

'You're utterly obsessed with the man,' said Harry grimly, and stood with arms folded. 'You said, again. Do you walk in your sleep often, may I ask?'

Her chin lifted. 'Only when I'm unhappy, I suppose. I did when I was a child, but I thought I'd grown out of it completely until I woke up recently to find myself in the muniment room in the middle of the night——'

'*What?* Why the hell didn't you tell me?' he asked, appalled, and moved nearer.

'I wasn't sure you'd be interested.'

'Interested!' Harry controlled himself with obvious effort. 'You could have fallen, broken a leg—anything could have happened.'

'Sleepwalkers rarely injure themselves, for some reason. Besides,' she added coldly, 'since I don't know myself when I'm about to walk in my sleep, I'm hardly in a position to inform anyone else.'

'What was so wrong about telling me when I was awake?'

'You haven't been exactly, well, encouraging regarding any personal confidences of mine lately, Harry, have you?'

There was a charged silence for several seconds while their eyes met and held, then Frances shivered, and Harry took her arm.

'Let's go,' he said shortly, and they went slowly down the aisle, Frances limping awkwardly and feeling chilled and miserable. So much for her intention to be sweet and loving, she thought, depressed, as Harry put out the lights and locked the door of the church. Then she gave a little squeak of surprise as he scooped her up and began walking with her towards the house.

'I'm too heavy to carry all the way back,' she protested. 'Really, Harry, you can't——'

'I can quite easily, but only if you shut up,' was the cavalier response. 'Conversation is out for the moment. I need my breath.' Harry was right. He was breathing very heavily indeed by the time he deposited Frances gently on her feet in the kitchen, his eyes filled with concern as he saw the pallor of her face. 'Are you really all right, Frances?'

She nodded, her eyes suspiciously bright. 'I'd just like to get to bed, I think.'

'Can you make it up the stairs with just a helping hand?' Harry managed the ghost of his old smile. 'You don't weigh much, but I can't guarantee to get you up there in one piece if I try to carry you all the way.'

She returned the smile gamely, 'Of course. Stairs are easy—I can grab the banisters as I go.'

Despite her brave words, Frances was profoundly thankful when, with Harry's help she finally negotiated the stairs and the bathroom and was safely installed in bed. She lay like a rag doll while Harry went downstairs to make her the tea she yearned for, too spent to care about anything much for the moment. When Harry returned she was amused to see the decanter alongside the teapot on the tray.

'The cure for all ills, Harry?'

'I wish it were. I can't say brandy's been much help to me lately, I'm afraid.' He smiled as he handed her a cup of tea. 'Nevertheless I have it on the best authority that it does wonders for a wrenched ankle.'

Harry went off to take a shower while Frances drank her tea, and she lay in dreamy comfort, the shock of her experience already fading now she was in her own bed. She was even able to summon up a warm smile when Harry came back in his dressing-gown, his hair slick with water. He poured a generous measure of brandy into two glasses and came over to stand looking down at her for a moment before he handed her one of the glasses and sat close to her on the bed.

'You look better,' he commented. 'How's the ankle?'

'It doesn't hurt at all now I'm lying down.' Frances sipped some of her brandy, feeling rather flustered by the steady regard of her husband's eyes at close quarters.

'I definitely thought you'd taken off, you know,' he said softly.

'Because of this morning?'

'I assumed it was the straw that broke the camel's back.'

'Are you alluding to me as a camel, by any chance?'

Harry grinned. 'You know perfectly well what I mean!'

'I would never leave without telling you, Harry,' said Frances carefully, then hesitated. 'Besides, aren't you forgetting something? I promised to give you a son if I could—remember?'

'It's not the sort of thing one forgets, Frances.' Harry put out a hand to touch hers. 'But I won't keep you to it. If you really are unhappy and want to leave me I won't stand in your way.'

Her eyes met his unwaveringly.

'I'd like to know what you feel on the subject, Harry? Do you want me to stay?'

Harry touched the tangled curls above her forehead with a gentle hand. 'If you like I'll go down on my knees and beg.'

His voice was so unemotional Frances found it hard to believe what she'd heard, and lay staring up at him, her mind in a turmoil. She would give her soul to have him beg her to stay, if he only knew it, but lacked the courage to say so as she tried to interpret the expression in Harry's eyes.

'It's the second time you've given me a shock at the thought of your departure,' he said conversationally. 'Remember the first time, when I played hell with you about the piece in the paper?'

'Vividly.'

'Yes, well, I soon came crawling to ask you to stay that time, if you remember. Tonight was ten times worse. I thought you'd already gone.'

'And you minded?'

'Minded? I went berserk—which is why I never thought

to look in your wardrobe to see if your clothes had gone—I just wasn't functioning normally.' Harry gave a short, mirthless laugh. 'I just ran round in ever-decreasing circles looking for you, then tore over to the gatehouse to see if Dolly had any idea where you were. She delivered a trenchant little lecture to me about looking after you better and sent Bates and me off to the the church, since that was the only place I hadn't looked. When I saw the lights on in there I felt sick with relief, until you weren't anywhere in sight when we opened the door. Then there you were like a ghost in that white frilly thing, with your eyes staring right through me as you hung on to Hal's railing like grim death. It was Bates who said you were asleep, and I was so relieved to hear it I lost my temper.'

'So I noticed,' observed Frances. 'For a moment there I thought you were about to break my neck.'

A genuine smile glimmered deep in Harry's eyes for the first time since he'd found her. 'I wanted to. So don't do it again.'

'I don't walk in my sleep from choice!'

His forehead creased in worried lines. 'How in heaven's name can I prevent it, Frances? Tell me what I can do!'

She thought it over carefully, and peeped at him from under her lashes. 'I can think of one or two things which might help.'

'Then tell me.'

'I'm fairly sure that if you held me in your arms all night I would *never* walk in my sleep.'

The corners of Harry's mouth twitched, and he leaned nearer. 'I think I could safely promise to manage that without much trouble. Any other suggestions?'

'If I thought you really loved me, Harry, and said so, in a way that convinced me you really didn't care for Annabel any more, I'm certain my sleepwalking days would be over for good,' Frances said in a rush, and looked away, the colour rushing into her cheeks.

Harry was silent for so long that Frances stole a look at him at last to find him staring at her in dumbfounded silence. Then he made an odd, choked noise deep in his throat and pulled her upright, holding her by the shoulders as he spoke very quickly and with great emphasis.

'I admit I was in love with Annabel once, but I never felt for her the way I feel about you. I love you, Frances, though it would only be honest to say I had no idea how much until the moment I slid this ring on your finger. For the rest of the wedding service I hardly heard a word the dean said because I was so cock-a-hoop with the realisation that I had you for my wife and how lucky I was. Which, I suppose is why I saw red when you muttered another man's name just when I thought we'd experienced—I don't know how to describe it. Does paradise sound a bit over the top?'

'No, exactly right,' she said breathlessly, then her eyes filled with tears and spilled over to run down her cheeks. 'Oh, Harry—don't punish me any more, I can't bear it!'

He snatched her into his arms and rubbed his face against hers over and over. 'Punish *you*,' he said unsteadily. 'It was myself I was punishing as well, and I just couldn't seem to find the words to put things right. Every day I'd get up and tell myself I'd grovel to you, beg forgiveness for being such a swine. Then I'd get to the breakfast table and there you'd be, enthroned behind the coffee tray without a hair out of place, looking as cool and aloof as an iceberg.'

Frances gave a little sob. 'Underneath I was a seething mass of tangled-up emotions, wanting to tell you I loved you, only you, and had from the moment you first made love to me that night.'

'What night?' he demanded, holding her so tight she began to wonder if her ribs would stand the strain.

'How many wedding-nights am I supposed to have had?' she asked pertly, and Harry smiled down at her in a way that flooded her with relief and happiness before his mouth was so occupied with kissing hers there were no more smiles or words for a long, breathless, ecstatic interval, while both of them tried to reassure each other of their true feelings without recourse to the English language to make themselves clear.

Harry raised his head after a while, grinning down at her in a way Frances had missed badly the past few weeks. 'When it comes to wedding nights, Mrs Curthoys, I'm afraid ours was the only one you're likely to experience, if I can help it. And I humbly apologise for wrecking it with my insane jealousy.'

Frances drew back, her eyes wide with delight. 'Oh, Harry,' she breathed blissfully. 'Were you really?'

'Jealous? Othello had nothing on me, I assure you. I still am jealous, if it comes to that,' he added gruffly.

Frances's eyes widened. 'Are you really, Harry?' she repeated, abruptly serious, and touched her hand to his cheek.

Harry caught the hand in his and kissed her fingers, his teeth catching each pink-nailed tip in emphasis. 'Until I met you, my heart, I'd never been jealous of anyone in my life—never even realised what an insidious, degrading feeling it can be. Now, I might tell you, I know precisely how Othello must have felt when he smothered Desdemona. I could only too easily have done the same to you when you muttered the wrong name that night.'

Frances gave a stifled protest that Harry silenced with a finger on her lips, his eyes deadly serious as they stared down into hers.

'I'm even jealous when I see you mooning over that miniature of Hal every night while you brush your hair at the mirror over there. I begrudge every moment you spend in thinking about him even, a man who's been dead for three hundred years, God help me!'

'Harry!'

'Hilarious, isn't it? Laugh if you want!'

Instead of laughing, Frances reached up to kiss him suddenly, surprising Harry even as he returned the kiss with interest.

'I'm glad,' she said fiercely.

'Glad?'

'Wonderfully, gloriously glad! If you can be jealous of a man who's dead, or even his miniature, then I know it's true. You *must* love me.'

Harry crushed her to him, rubbing his cheek over and over again against hers. 'It's the incontrovertible truth, Frances Curthoys.'

She drew back to look at him, her eyes luminous.

'But I do love the miniature just the same, Harry. But not because it's Hal. The reason I'm so attached to it is that it reminds me of you.' A look of such incredulous delight dawned in Harry's eyes that Frances was affected deeply, and laughed shakily to disguise it. 'You know how Shakespeare described a miniature like this, Harry? He called it "the manacle of love".'

'If that means I have you chained to me for the rest of our lives then I think he was on the right track—though manacles sound a bit kinky, sweetheart!' The old, gleaming smile was back in Harry's eyes at long last, and Frances relaxed against him in utter relief.

'But let's get something straight, Harry Curthoys,' she said with severity. 'Let's have no more talk of jealousy— about Chris, poor Hal, or anyone else, living or dead. You have no need to be jealous—ever.'

'Do you really mean that, Frances?'

'Of course——' Whatever else she had in mind to say was stifled as Harry's mouth came down on hers with such hunger that she hardly knew what he was talking about when, some time later, he asked if her ankle was troubling her.

'What ankle?' she answered, gazing up at him, and Harry laughed breathlessly.

'In that case, darling, I have a suggestion to make.'

She wriggled closer. 'Yes?'

'It probably sounds odd, under the circumstances—I mean, I know very well you've let me make love to you all along——'

'*Let* you? Is that what I was doing?'

Harry shook her slightly. 'Listen to me, woman. I'm trying to be serious.'

'Sorry. Go on.'

'I just had this idea that we could look on tonight as our

real wedding night, because now we know how each other feels—only I'm frankly astounded that you're capable of loving me at all, after the way I've treated you lately.'

'Very true. But I do love you. Warts and all,' she assured him lovingly.

'Hey, steady on. That was Cromwell. The Curthoys family have always been strictly Royalist.'

'Don't I know it.' Frances shivered and burrowed her face against him. 'I dreamed Hal was trying to take me with him tonight, Harry.'

His arms tightened protectively. 'Put him out of your mind, darling. He had his chance, poor chap, and he chose the wrong girl. I almost did the same, but I was given a second chance, thank God, when I found you, Frances Curthoys, and I'm hanging on to you. Forget about statues in future and concentrate on your flesh and blood husband.'

She slid a hand inside his dressing-gown, smoothing his warm skin with pleasure. 'And deliriously happy I am with the arrangement. You needn't warn me off marble effigies, Harry. After tonight my enthusiasm for them has rather evaporated.'

Harry reached out to turn off the light before sliding down beside his wife in the wide bed, pulling her close with a deep sigh. 'There,' he said in her ear. 'You won't get away from me tonight, I promise you.'

'I shan't want to. It's where I want to be, Harry, tonight and every night.' She stretched against him, luxuriating in their restored harmony, and smiled into the darkness, deciding that now was the perfect time to tell her husband a piece of news she had been keeping to herself for some time. 'Harry,' she began.

'Mm?' he murmured inattentively, his lips against her throat.

Frances wriggled in delight, but pushed him away a little, determined not to be sidetracked. 'I've been waiting for ages to hit on the right moment to give you a rather interesting piece of news, Harry . . .'

* * *

On a bright sunlit afternoon just before the following Easter the church at Curthoys Court was once again decked wih flowers from altar to font, this time for the christening of Nicholas Edward Francis Henry Curthoys. Since the godfathers, including Edward Napier, RA, professed themselves nervous to a man of the honour, young Nicholas lay placidly in the arms of his doting godmother and aunt, Mrs James Colville, as the group clustered round the font to watch the rector sprinkle holy water on the small pink face, which emitted a single incensed wail in response to the indignity.

'Letting the devil out,' pronounced his grandmother with satisfaction after the service was over, and held out her arms. 'Right, Charlotte, you've had him long enough. Hand him over.'

'It's quite a step to the house, honey,' said her husband anxiously, 'you feel tired and you give him to me now, you hear?'

Harry chuckled as he lagged behind a little with Frances when the christening party was walking back to the house for a celebration lunch. 'Dexter will have to fight Dolly tooth and nail for the privilege, don't you think? Look at the way she's hovering at Mother's shoulder.'

Frances smiled as she watched. 'I'm glad Dolly's so happy to be in charge of the nursery again. Once everything was reorganised, with Bates's niece Alison in charge of the kitchen, and all the extra help for the house, she actually admitted it had all been getting a trifle too much for her.'

Harry let out a great sigh of thanksgiving. 'I can't believe it's all happened sometimes. You, I mean, then young Nick, and the money——'

'Not to mention the new roof!'

'My God, no, let's not forget the new roof!' He paused to kiss her and Eddy Napier turned from chatting up Jassy to shout at them.

'Come on, you two. Less of the canoodling—I'm hungry.'

'You are unfailingly vulgar, Edward Napier,' said

Caroline Napier severely. 'I can't think why Frances let you stand as godfather,'

'Because I painted such a superlative portrait of her, dearest sister-in-law,' said Eddy loftily. 'No other Curthoys bride has ever been portrayed with such supreme mastery, I assure you.'

'Hey now,' protested Dexter Bancroft. 'I'm sure you've done a great job on your picture of Frances, young fellow, but it'll have to be something mighty special to beat the one Harry was kind enough to give me of Nadine.'

'Oh, Dexter,' remonstrated his wife, laughing, and surrendered her burden reluctantly to Dolly. 'Anyway, Harry, when are we to see this famous portrait? Have you hung it up in the gallery?'

'No fear!' Harry smiled smugly. 'It's over the fireplace in the morning-room where I can look at it as much as I like. What's the point in banishing my wife up to the gallery where no one sees the picture except the visitors?'

The guests were provided with champagne as Dolly bore the baby off to be changed into something more comfortable than his antique lace christening robe, and then Harry ushered everyone into the morning-room where a sheet hung over the portrait on the chimney breast. With due ceremony he reached up and unveiled the painting, which was greeted with a moment's complete silence before Matt Wilding cleared his throat and stepped forward to shake Eddy Napier by the hand.

'Congratulations. You were right. Superlative describes it exactly.'

Eddy gave an expansive bow, lapping up the praise heaped on him from all sides. Frances gazed up at her likeness, hardly able to believe, even now, that the beautiful young woman in the portrait was really herself.

Eddy had painted her seated in a winged chair. The faded green tapestry made a perfect background for the subtle pink of her silk dress and dark sheen of her hair which curled softly against her cheek and neck as she leaned slightly over the baby lying on her lap. One hand touched the string of pearls Harry had given her when their son was born, not waiting for today, their first anniversary, and she looked up from beneath slightly raised brows in the portrait, as though the onlooker had just distracted her attention from her son.

'A slight departure from the rule,' said Nadine softly, and smiled at her triumphant son. 'Was it your idea, Harry to have young Nick in the picture too?'

'No. I just wanted Frances,' he said simply, and squeezed the hand his wife slid into his.

'Young Frances refused to sit for me unless she could cuddle her son while she was doing it,' complained Eddy. 'New territory for me, babies.'

'You've caught him beautifully,' said Jassy, admiringly. 'Just look at his perfect little fingernails.'

'Never mind the fingernails,' said Eddy, aggrieved. 'Just turn your attention to the lace on that blasted christening robe. That precise age-yellowed tint is murder to reproduce—I sweated blood over it.'

'Not in vain, young man,' observed Mr Godfrey Dangerfield, and resorted to his monocle to examine the portrait in detail. 'Damn pretty girl, Frances. You're a fortunate man, Harry my boy. Portrait must have set you back a packet, though—I hear an Edward Napier original don't come cheap these days.'

'This one does,' contradicted Eddy gloomily. 'It's my wedding present to Frances and Harry.'

'Bit behind, aren't you?' said his brother, grinning.

'Not my fault. Should have painted it ages ago, but Harry put me off. Said they were going off on honeymoon, would you believe. It was months after the wedding.'

'Frances needed a change,' said Harry blandly, and shepherded the guests towards the dining-room. 'She'd been working flat out on the Curthoys archives, so I thought it seemed rather a good idea to nip off to Antigua for a week or two and lie in the sun. Now, if you'll all go in I'm sure Eddy and Matt will provide you with more champagne while Frances and I just check on our son for a moment.' With a brilliant smile at the assembled company he whisked Frances from the room and ran with her to the library and closed the door firmly.

'I thought we were off to check on Nick,' protested Frances, laughing, as Harry pulled her into his arms.

'Our son is perfectly happy with Dolly for the moment, but his father just couldn't exist a moment longer without telling his gorgeous mother how much he loves her before they join the party.' And Harry removed his wife's elegant hat and threw it carelessly on the table before kissing Frances with such exuberance she had no alternative but to respond in kind, and it was some time before he let her go. 'Are you glad you married me after all?' he asked, rubbing his cheek against hers.

'I always have been, Harry. Even when you were an out and out pig to me there were, well, compensations.'

Harry laughed softly and held her closer. 'Poor old Hal. I don't suppose he ever had this.'

'Perhaps he did in the beginning.'

'Until Arabella fell for the doctor.' He raised her face to his. 'You don't have a yen for Dr Nicholson, by any chance?'

Her eyes were lambent with her unspoken answer and Harry groaned softly and bent to kiss her. 'I wish we didn't have guests for lunch——'

'But you do,' said an amused voice from the doorway. 'And the sooner you feed us the sooner you'll be rid of us.' Nadine stood laughing, her eyes soft as they rested on her son and the flushed girl in his arms. 'I think you've had quite long enough to see your son, you deceitful boy. Come and toast your baby, *and* the clever wife who presented him to you so promptly.'

Frances smiled reminiscently. 'His father's first words to him were, "By God, young Curthoys, are we pleased to see you! Happy New Year", which surprised the ward sister no end.'

'Since you came into my life, darling, New Year's Eve has become a lucky date for me,' said Harry. 'Young Nick arrived on the stroke of midnight this year, and the year before that was quite memorable too.' He grinned down at Frances meaningfully, then held out his free arm to his mother as they went to join the others.

Frances chuckled. 'What do you have in mind for next New Year's Eve, then?'

'A granddaughter would be nice,' suggested Nadine slyly, and the assembled company in the dining-room looked up in surprise as their host arrived in gales of laughter as he settled his ladies in their places.

The ensuing luncheon party was a lively affair which lasted long into the afternoon, and by the time the last guest had finally gone, and young Nicholas Curthoys was settled down for the night, it was very late before his parents could relax alone together in peace over a tray of leftovers, while Mrs Bates kept watch upstairs.

Harry drew the cork from a bottle of champagne kept back from lunch, and filled two glasses. 'Now we're alone I'd like to propose a private toast of my own, sweetheart.' He sat down beside Frances on the sofa and put an arm round her, drawing her close.

'What shall it be?' she asked, sighing contentedly.

'I've been thinking over Mother's suggestion earlier on, about producing a granddaughter for her next New Year's Eve,' he said, poker-faced.

Frances twisted in his arms to look up at him, her eyes dancing. 'Really!'

'In which case I suggest we drink a toast to—March the thirty-first.' His grey eyes gleamed down as her with an audacity that prompted a sharp dig in the ribs from his loving spouse.

'Very well.' Frances raised her glass. 'To March the thirty-first, then. Significant, I assume, because it's our son's christening day, also our first wedding anniversary——'

'And,' broke in Harry, as he pulled her to her feet, 'by sheer coincidence, dear heart, it also happens to be nine months to the day—or night—to next New Year's Eve!'

As Frances and Harry Curthoys climbed the stairs, arms

around each other, their mingled laughter carried softly through the house, muted, plangent echoes of their mirth reaching as far as the long gallery, where moonlight played on the portrait of Hal Curthoys, giving an illusion of warmth to the sombre painted eyes, as though Hal heard the joyous sound and was glad.

Coming Next Month

Available in November wherever paperback books are sold, or through
Harlequin Reader Service:

In the U.S.
901 Fuhrmann Blvd.
P.O. Box 1397
Buffalo, N.Y. 14240-1397

In Canada
P.O. Box 603
Fort Erie, Ontario
L2A 5X3

What the press says about Harlequin romance fiction...

"When it comes to romantic novels...
Harlequin is the indisputable king."
—*New York Times*

"...always with an upbeat, happy ending."
—*San Francisco Chronicle*

"Women have come to trust these
stories about contemporary people,
set in exciting foreign places."
—*Best Sellers*, New York

"The most popular reading matter of
American women today."
— *Detroit News*

"...a work of art."
— *Globe & Mail*, Toronto

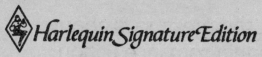

Harlequin Signature Edition

Penny Jordan

Stronger Than Yearning

He was the man of her dreams!

The same dark hair, the same mocking eyes; it was as if the
Regency rake of the portrait, the seducer of Jenna's dream, had
come to life. Jenna, believing the last of the Deverils dead, was
determined to buy the great old Yorkshire Hall—to claim it for
her daughter, Lucy, and put to rest some of the painful memo-
ries of Lucy's birth. She had no way of knowing that a direct descendant of the black sheep Deveril even existed—or that James
Allingham and his own powerful yearnings would disrupt her
plan entirely.

Penny Jordan's first Harlequin Signature Edition *Love's Choices* was an
outstanding success. Penny Jordan has written more than 40 best-sell-
ing titles—more than 4 million copies sold.

Now, be sure to buy her latest bestseller, *Stronger Than Yearning*. Available wherever paperbacks are sold—in October.

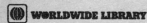